"I don't need anything from you."

To Daniel who was struggling with the swirl of needs Markie had aroused, the statement was a challenge.

"I wasn't offering," he said coldly. "I was about to say that if you need anything, don't look to me for help."

Markie flushed inwardly, but gave no outward sign of distress. "I won't bother you while I'm here."

Daniel's gaze drifted disdainfully over her slender form, taking in the worn jeans and shirt. "You couldn't," he assured her, feeling the invisible barriers rise. "As long as you stay out of my sight, we shouldn't have any problems."

Markie didn't know why she felt compelled to challenge this man. She suspected it had something to do with the unfamiliar emotions he evoked in her.

Books by Morgan Patterson

HARLEQUIN ROMANCE
2667—DARKER FIRE

Don't miss any of our special offers. Write to us at the
following address for information on our newest releases.

Harlequin Reader Service
P.O. Box 1397, Buffalo, NY 14240
Canadian address: P.O. Box 603,
Fort Erie, Ont. L2A 5X3

MORGAN PATTERSON

wild flower wind

Harlequin Books

TORONTO • NEW YORK • LONDON
AMSTERDAM • PARIS • SYDNEY • HAMBURG
STOCKHOLM • ATHENS • TOKYO • MILAN

To my sisters—
Marilyn, who reaches for the
dream of romance
and Janine, who holds the
reality of love.

Harlequin Presents first edition May 1991
ISBN 0-373-11366-8

Original hardcover edition published in 1990
by Mills & Boon Limited

WILD FLOWER WIND

PROLOGUE

HE FOUND her sleeping in a meadow of wild flowers—golden pea and violets and wild hyacinth tumbling together in a riot of colour. It hardly seemed to matter that it was *his* meadow, land that he guarded as jealously as he guarded himself. Oddly, it seemed as if she belonged there, soft and somehow fragile, like the flowers, despite the fact that some of them were rooted in solid granite.

He watched her for a long time, from his position on the ground beside her. Sunlight danced across the field, shadow and light playing chase across them both. Even in sleep, he thought in wonder, she seemed so *alive*. Like the flowers, she was colour and light and all of springtime.

He watched intently as a playful breeze tugged a strand of dark hair across her forehead, a soft shadow marking her creamy skin. Without thought, without volition, he reached his hand out to tuck the strand away. The very tips of his fingers slid across her temple. He might as well have danced in flames, so searing was the sensation that shook him. Snatching his hand away, the man studied this newest flower warily. His mind told him to leave now, to walk away and not look back. Other parts of him, parts long since quiet and thought mastered, told him to stay. To stay and find the source of the flame.

In silence, he fought the battle. Finally, with a grim expression, he squared his shoulders and made to rise to his feet. He was going to walk away. He would turn his back to the flame and face the cold.

Then she opened her eyes.

They were emerald-green, and the first glance laid bare his soul. He could *feel* those eyes. An overwhelming and long familiar protective instinct rose, prompting a grim defence.

'This is private property!'

CHAPTER ONE

MARKIE, waking from a peaceful rest, stared at the man kneeling beside her. She wondered if she should be afraid, then dismissed the thought. It was a typical Markie decision. She had overcome fear of the unknown long ago.

Now, as always, Markie relied on her instincts. Yes, she saw the power in him, physical and emotional. And she saw the strength as well. He looked as hard as the mountains surrounding them and as unforgiving, and yet. . . Deciding that clarification was called for, she caught him unaware and—smiled.

'Hello.'

He blinked. There was nothing else to betray him.

'My name is Markie,' she continued quietly, sitting up. 'What's yours?'

Daniel shook his head slowly. 'Didn't you hear me? This is private property——'

'Yours?'

'Mine,' he confirmed, his voice ringing with possession.

'Good. I would have had to track you down later today anyway.'

'What for?' His voice was wary.

'To ask if I could camp here, of course,' Markie explained in surprise, her tone somehow indicating that he was none too bright.

'You don't seem to understand,' he told her succinctly. 'This is private property. It's not a campground.'

'I don't see a fence,' challenged Markie, her eyes challenging as well.

Daniel shifted uncomfortably. There was no fence. He had never quite been able to put that fence up, to enclose all nature's beauty and claim it for his own. Yes, he held the deed and he had paid the price—how he had paid!—but somehow he had never taken the last step of erecting the physical barrier that would demand recognition from the world. . .and himself. Had it not been for his overwhelming need for solitude, he doubted that he would have even been able to put up the sparsely posted signs warning trespassers away. But that was a principle for him to wrestle with, not a point to be debated with this. . .wild flower.

'My land,' he repeated harshly.

'Don't be silly,' she dismissed airily. 'You know it's no more yours than mine. I won't hurt it in any way, I promise. No trash, no scavenging wood for a camp-fire. Look, I didn't even hurt the wild flowers.' Her small, capable hand swept out over the immediate area, indicating the place where she had slept. She had been careful in choosing her spot not to crush the delicate blooms.

'You don't need to worry about the wild flowers,' Daniel told her softly, his eyes riveted on her face. 'They only look fragile. Some take root in. . .the most unlikely places.'

Markie studied him critically. She had no idea what had brought that thoughtful, wary expression to his face. The statement was innocuous enough, and yet. . .

She tilted her head, as though to study him from a new angle. 'Trespassing, your type would say. Maybe you should build that fence.'

His gaze sharpened on her face. 'You're wrong,' he told her bluntly. 'On all counts. Trespass is intrusion without permission. And I'm not a *type* of man.'

Their eyes held in silence. Again, Markie received the same dizzying impression of strength and single-mindedness as when she had first awakened. But now she also felt the force of an *individual*, a man who blazed his own trails and asked, wanted, needed no one to follow.

In accepting that, she experienced a sense of recognition. She knew this man intimately, without knowing a single fact about him. She wanted, suddenly, to know more.

'Wild flowers don't ask permission,' she reminded him quietly. 'I am asking.'

His eyes narrowed. 'Where did you come from?'

Markie smiled at him carelessly to hide the sudden slash of pain. 'As I understand it, a mommy and daddy loved each other very much and one day decided that they could love a little baby too——'

'Are we working our way to the stork or the cabbage patch?' Daniel interrupted, seemingly unamused.

With a small grin Markie conceded the skirmish, gesturing gracefully to the backpack propped against a nearby pine. 'I hiked in.'

Daniel studied the well-used piece of equipment critically. 'I assume you crossed over from the National Forest?'

'That's where I started out.'

'It adjoins my land,' he explained absently, eyes curious. 'How long have you been hiking?'

'On this particular trip?' she asked, considering. 'Four or five days.'

'That looks like a pretty heavy pack. And this is rough country.' His eyes moved lazily over her lovely face and slender form, measuring. 'You don't seem the type.'

She met his gaze coolly. 'You're wrong—on all counts. Like the wild flowers, I can survive in the most unlikely places. And I'm not a *type* of woman.'

The challenge was clear. She had echoed his previous sentiment, if not his exact words, directly back at him. No, she was not a *type* of woman. He had known from the instant she had opened those emerald eyes that she would not fit into any comfortable category. There was such life—such vibrant, hungry life—inside her, and flashes of so much more that he had seen only briefly. Wariness and determination, joy and fear, challenge and serenity, he had seen them all in the short time he had spent with her.

And there was something else, something she had just said about being like the wild flowers. . .that she could survive in unlikely places. But she had not said that she could take root. It seemed a deliberate evasion, a careful pronouncement, and suddenly he needed to know why.

'Are you alone?' he demanded abruptly.

'And if I am?'

He weighed her wariness. 'I just want to know what to expect in the way of company.'

She examined him minutely before answering. 'I'm alone.'

Daniel nodded. He hadn't really expected any other answer. The independence he had seen flash in her eyes seemed deeply rooted and long held. 'A dangerous way to travel,' he observed.

Markie's voice went cool. 'I can take care of myself.'

'What if you got hurt, or sick, in the middle of nowhere?'

'I can take care of myself.'

Daniel tried another tack. 'You're on vacation, I suppose?'

'Do you?' She smiled insouciantly, and he was suddenly inundated with an overwhelming desire to taste that smile.

'Do I what?' he managed blankly, trying to deal with the unexpected and consuming desire.

'Do you suppose?'

That snapped him back to grim reality. 'Do you always talk like this?'

'Like what?'

'In questions,' he clarified irritably. 'In challenges. That's all this conversation has been from beginning to end!'

It was an insight that captured Markie's attention. Most people never perceived it, the distance she maintained through humour and evasion. It was a lesson she had learned early in life, one she had thought she had mastered. Yet it had taken this man less than ten minutes to see through the mask.

'Yes,' she answered at length, meeting his eyes, 'I always talk like this.'

In the silence that followed her admission, Daniel studied Markie closely. The statement hadn't been bitter, or angry, although in some way he thought it should have been. Instead the words had been wry, carrying the strength of self-knowledge.

He was abruptly torn. He wanted to find her answers and he wanted to protect himself from the involvement that tugged at him. 'If I deny you permission to camp here——?'

'Are you?'

Daniel met her measuring gaze in silence before releasing a pent-up sigh. 'No,' he backed down abruptly, curiosity winning over self-protection, 'I'm not. You can make camp here.'

Markie watched as he shifted restlessly, seeing a kind of self-directed impatience in him. True to form, she said nothing, more occupied with observing than commenting.

'You have a tent——?'

Since his gaze was focused somewhere over her left shoulder, Markie supplied a simple, 'Yes.'

'If there's anything——'

'No.' She issued the denial before the offer was even made, and silently berated herself as he turned sharp eyes her way. It was a hang-up left from her childhood, she knew, refusing assistance before it could be offered, denying the need to ever take the help of another. But knowing the source of the problem and controlling it were two very different things. 'I don't need anything from you.'

To Daniel, who was struggling with the elusive swirl of needs Markie had aroused, the statement was cold challenge. His eyes iced over and his shoulders squared. 'I wasn't offering,' he said coldly. 'I was about to say that if you need anything, don't look to me for help.'

Markie flinched inwardly, but gave no outward sign of distress—another childhood hold-over. 'I won't bother you while I'm here.'

Daniel allowed his gaze to drift disdainfully over her slender form, taking in the worn jeans and faded shirt. 'You couldn't,' he assured her, feeling the invisible barriers rise. 'As long as you stay out of my sight, we shouldn't have any problem.'

With a brusque nod of his head he turned away. He had taken perhaps half a dozen steps when he suddenly stopped. Markie studied his stiff back curiously, wondering what had made him pause.

He turned back jerkily, as though in response to some unseen force. The question he threw at her was abrupt to the point of coldness. 'What did you mean, earlier, when you said that I no more owned this land than you did?'

Markie shrugged carelessly to hide her interest in his

response. 'I understand how people can own cars, and houses. But I just can't seem to accept the theory that a person can own trees and streams, lakes and. . .wild flowers.' She laughed with light derision. 'I mean, who do you buy something like that from? What do you pay for it?'

Daniel studied her in silence, eyes intent, as though looking for a clue to an unsolved puzzle.

Markie watched the frown between his dark brows deepen as she quietly waited for his response. The few people with whom she had shared her views had treated her as if she were ever so slightly unbalanced. The usual response was a detailed lecture on the free enterprise system and general scorn for the practicality of respecting nature. The reaction didn't bother Markie, because she used it as a kind of test, taking the measure of the individual through his reaction. There had been very few she'd cared enough for, or been curious enough about, to test. She didn't know why she had felt compelled to challenge this man, but she had the painful suspicion that it had something to do with the unfamiliar emotions he evoked inside her.

His response, when it came after minutes of silence, told her more than any discourse she had heard to date. He said nothing at all, but Markie noticed that the frown had disappeared.

'How long do you think you'll be staying?' he asked.

She smiled just a bit grimly and answered softly, 'Until I leave.'

One dark brow arched sardonically. 'Is your whole life that whimsical?'

"Whimsical?' she mused ironically, thinking of her childhood. 'I wouldn't call it that.'

'What would you call it?'

'Practical,' she answered evenly. 'I'll stay until I leave. What is it in that statement that you find confusing?'

'In the statement?' His eyes narrowed. 'Nothing. In you. . .?'

She met his eyes carefully, determined he would find no clues on her face. 'You never told me your name,' she reminded him.

Daniel's mouth twisted. 'No, I didn't.'

Without another word, without another challenge, he turned and strode from the meadow.

Markie watched him leave with a strange mixture of regret and relief. There was something about him, something about the searing perception in his eyes or the edge that balanced his questions, that made her strangely uneasy.

Well, she didn't need his approval. She had never needed anyone's approval. All her life she had walked alone, made her own way, and she would continue to do so.

As a child she had lived by other people's rules, pandered to other people's priorities. But she was a woman now, and in charge of her life. There was something inside Markie that would not let her settle to any other standard than her own. . .and her own was demanding. The memories of her past made it so.

Markie's very earliest memory was of a young woman with sad, resentful eyes. She was pretty, in that way raw stones are pretty until sharpened and refined into beauty. There seemed to be a flaw in her, though, a weakness that would preclude surviving the process intact.

The woman had been her mother. And when Markie was three, her mother had released her into the custody of the State of Texas. Markie remembered everything very clearly after that point. Every one of the thirteen foster homes she had lived in had remained etched in her mind, although truthfully they all seemed the same after a while—parents, children, some related, but most not, in a loose collection of humanity that could better be described as a convenience than a family. She grew to expect that she would be removed from the home the second she began to feel she could find a place for herself there, and so quickly learned to belong only within herself. Even as a child, Markie had known that was something they could not take away from her, although at times they seemed determined to try.

In between times, when there were no families to stay with, she remained in State custody, housed in facilities that sometimes served as detention centres and shelters as well. Early on, Markie saw how ugly life could be, how painful and empty and sad. And early on, she determined that her life would not follow that pattern.

With gritty determination, she had fought her way past the bitterness that could have trapped her in that other life. Determined that somehow, somewhere, she would find the place where she belonged, she made it through every foster home and institution. At the age of eight she discovered books and lost herself in their beauty. To her, the written word became first an escape and then a place, where she could find a million other worlds. History was a passion, science a fascination, fiction an obsession. Even encyclopaedias were a joy to Markie as she worked her way through the library. What had started as an evasion became a goal, and she knew by the age of twelve what she was meant to be.

The scars she carried from her childhood were all inside and well hidden. The one that manifested itself most often was a steely determination to make her own way without help. All her victories, all her defeats, would be her own. And unlike her mother, the responsibility for them would be her own as well. By far the deepest scar was the one that kept her moving, but that was one even Markie wouldn't acknowledge.

From the time she was old enough to understand that she would ultimately be responsible for her life, she had determined that there would be no place in her future for bitterness. She had seen too many of her fellow foster-children ruined, broken, destroyed by it. What she had hated most in her childhood—dependence, duty, charity, displacement—she vowed to sweep from her life. For six years she had struggled to become a woman free of those destructive traits. Now, at twenty-four, she was independent of everyone and everything. She had deliberately chosen a career that made her responsible to no one except herself. What she owed, she owed only to herself. She needed nothing that she couldn't achieve alone, although she was painfully aware that some things came harder than others. When she found her place, when she truly belonged, she would have conquered every ghost from her childhood. . .except the loneliness. And that, she mused, was something she would live with. Deep down, Markie was aware that loneliness was the one thing that couldn't be conquered alone. . .

She pulled herself from her distracted musings. She had more practical matters to concentrate on, and practicality demanded all her resources. She was, unfortunately, not a practical woman. She possessed less than an ounce of common sense, relying instead on her natural intelligence. Somehow, though, things always turned out right, so she didn't worry overmuch about this lack in her make-up.

Standing, Markie surveyed the meadow with an experienced eye, looking for the best place to pitch her tent. She searched for flat, rock-free ground where she wouldn't damage the wild flowers. Her landlord had made his feelings on that issue quite clear.

The tent was easy to assemble, and she had it up in no time. Since she tended to get claustrophobic in the single models, she carried a tent that slept two. This gave her room to move around and bring any extra gear inside for protection from the elements. When disassembled, though, the tent folded into a ridiculously tiny pouch and weighed next to nothing. Markie silently saluted the miracle of nylon.

Around six o'clock her camp was set up, and she cast a wary look at the sky. It was beginning to cloud up, the beautiful spring day dwindling towards a grey evening.

Grey. . .like his eyes.

Markie shook her head impatiently. She had to stop thinking about her reluctant landlord and concentrate instead on herself. She would have a quick dinner now and then retire for the night. There certainly wouldn't be much for her to do outside if a rainstorm moved in, as the sky threatened.

Suddenly Markie shivered. The temperature was dropping with the sun, reminding her how early in spring it really was. The day had been almost summer-like, but she wasn't fooled. Summer didn't come to the mountains this early, or this easily. As with all things of beauty, half the joy of summer lay in the struggle to achieve it.

She pulled on her jacket and lay back on the ground, a bag of trail mix at her side. It wasn't much of a dinner, but she had run through her supply of fresh food a couple of days before. She didn't really mind. Food ranked low on her list of priorities, certainly after solitary days and beautiful sunsets.

She lost track of time, lying there, watching the day

fade away. Time seemed to be passing so quickly lately, weeks turning into months as she drifted, moving from place to place. Markie sighed. She had lost track of all the sunsets she had watched and all the places she had watched them from. Some day, she promised herself in familiar refrain. Some day she would watch every sunset from her home.

But for now, here, the sun was gone and she was tired, despite the early hour. The last few days had included some hard hiking, and she could use a long night of sleep. Brushing her hands over the soft grass, she pushed herself up and moved to her tent. Out of habit, she scanned the area with a critical eye, checking to see that everything was well secured. The wind was picking up, causing her to shiver again. Before this trip, she hadn't known how cold the nights got in the Rockies. Tonight looked as if it would be the coldest yet. Her heavy sleeping-bag would be worth its weight in gold.

Once in the tent, Markie cast a regretful eye at her notebook, knowing that she was too tired to work. Instead, she burrowed into her sleeping-bag, happily unaware that the dropping temperature would be the least of her worries.

CHAPTER TWO

MARKIE had long since surrendered to sleep by the time the first snowflakes began to fall. Curled as she was into the downy warmth of her sleeping-bag, her only acknowledgement of the falling temperatures was unconscious as her body tightened in search of warmth, the cold invading her dreams.

But Daniel was awake. For over an hour he had watched the sky, uncertain of nature's mood but aware that something was about to go awry. For a while he convinced himself that it was only his reaction to Markie's invasion that troubled him, preventing him from settling to any task.

God, yes, she troubled him. He had somehow taken for granted that his privacy was inviolable, his wherever he was. He had built no fences around his land because he had built far more effective barriers around himself. He hadn't thought they could be challenged by anything or anyone. He had forgotten to take wild flowers into account.

He had convinced himself that these years spent in the mountains were the end of a journey. He had struggled long and hard to learn life's lessons, and he had absorbed what he learned. It led him to these mountains, where he could write and think and explore without being touched by that other life, the one that insisted on repeating its lessons over and over again. Once was enough for Daniel. He had learned and become invulnerable. Or so he had thought. . . Yes, years ago he had ended one journey in these mountains. Now it appeared that he was about to begin another.

Shaking his head at fate's sense of humour, Daniel turned his eyes absently to the horizon. All impractical thoughts fled from his mind. He had been so occupied mapping out an unseen and uncertain future that he had failed to observe the changing weather. With a muffled curse he studied the approaching front.

The weather in the Rockies was a wondrous and wild thing, as unexpected as any woman. It wasn't unusual to see a beautiful early spring day such as this one end with a snowstorm. Mother Nature was a tricky woman. The clouds rolling up from the distance were leaden with snow, dark and threatening against an early evening sky turned a shade of pale yellow peculiar to heavy snowfall.

Daniel crossed to his radio and switched it on, easily tuning in on the weather advisory station. The storm was moving in rapidly from the north where it had already dumped feet—*feet*—of snow in the high country. Contrary to all hopes, it was gathering force as it moved southward. Daniel calculated that it would hit his corner of the Rockies within two hours.

And Markie was camped in his meadow, among his wild flowers, half an hour's hike away. Daniel's jaw tightened.

'Damn!'

She wasn't familiar with the land. He didn't know if she would be able to fend for herself. She had no idea where his house was, and he had made it quite plain that the house was off limits even if she did stumble across it.

His shoulders squared. He would have to go after her and bring her back to wait out the storm. It was the only option. With automatic efficiency, he began gathering the materials he would need: coat, gloves and boots were joined by an extra pair of gloves, a backpack with an adequate supply of medical materials, rope, water, food, flashlight, and a small flask of brandy. These he gathered with the long practice and unthinking skill of an experienced hiker.

Cursing fate, and his own over-developed sense of responsibility for wild flowers left to flounder in an early spring snow, Daniel started on his trek. The combined darkness of the gathering night and the approaching front made his progress much slower than normal. He knew that when the storm had passed and the mountains were left blanketed with snow even the blackest night would seem like day. But at those times the mountains were at their most treacherous, with blankets of virginal white hiding danger.

As he made his way to the meadow, Daniel strained his eyes searching for signs of Markie. Broken branches, overturned rocks, crushed grass, footprints in the softer soil—he found nothing. Which meant, he decided, one of two things. Either she had not left her campsite in the meadow or she had headed in the opposite direction. All things considered, Daniel hoped desperately for the first option. His house was the only shelter to be found for miles. If Markie had gone in the opposite direction, he had no doubt that he would still be tracking her when the full force of the storm hit. And then they would both be stranded and at its mercy.

He was halfway to the meadow when the first light flakes began to fall. Twenty minutes had passed since he had left his home. He calculated that they could make it back to safety just in time. . .if Markie had not left camp and if nothing delayed them on the way. Two big 'ifs', Daniel conceded, but at the moment he wasn't ready to face the alternative.

When he reached the edge of the meadow, he stopped to allow air to regulate once again in his lungs. He had pushed himself relentlessly on the hike down so that they might have extra time for the trek back.

In the distance, against the backdrop of night and light snowfall, he could just make out the outlines of Markie's tent. With a silent sigh of relief, he straightened and picked his way across a rocky part of the meadow towards the tent.

At the entrance he stared into it, unable to make out even the slightest details in the gloom. Finding his flashlight, he clicked it on and covered the light with spread fingers, muting its glare.

The light picked out the sleeping-bag immediately, its occupant curled tightly against the cold. Daniel smiled wryly. She must have been exhausted, despite her earlier nap. She hadn't even awakened. She wasn't aware of the danger she was in.

Dropping to his knees, Daniel crawled into the mouth of the tent. With the aid of his flashlight he studied Markie's peaceful features. He somehow didn't think she was the type to appreciate being awakened by a strange man in the middle of nowhere during a snowstorm. But then again, he reassured himself blithely, you never could tell about these things. She might like it.

She didn't. He had barely stretched one hand forward to shake her awake when she spoke.

'Before you proceed,' she began in a steady, controlled tone that broke through the darkness, 'I think it's only fair to warn you that I have a blue belt in Tae Kwondo. That's one below a brown, which is one below a black, which means I could hurt you if I had to.'

Daniel tried, but didn't quite manage, to muffle his laughter. 'If I were intent on assaulting you I'd have done it earlier, before the snowstorm.'

At the first sound of his familiar voice, Markie bolted upright, knocking the flashlight from his hand. The light played wildly against the nylon of the tent before settling blankly against one side.

'You!' Markie grasped his arm, squeezing tightly as if to assure herself of his presence. 'Dammit, you scared me!'

Daniel patted her hand awkwardly, manfully ignoring the fact that she was cutting off the blood supply to his arm. 'I didn't mean to frighten you.'

'Well, that certainly explains why you came sneaking into my tent in the middle of the night, then, doesn't it?' Because her pulse was still shuddering, the sarcasm didn't quite come off.

Daniel forbore mentioning that it was barely eight o'clock in the evening, too busy studying her in the faint light from the flashlight. Her hair was tousled with sleep, her face flushed. Those wonderful green eyes were bright, with a trace of lingering drowsiness softening the fire.

Suddenly in those eyes he saw a sharpening comprehension. 'Snowstorm?' she repeated carefully.

'Atta girl!' he praised ironically.

Without any verbal warning, Markie scrambled to her knees and crawled to the opening of the tent. On the way, she overturned a lantern and trampled Daniel.

'It's snowing!' she told him in amazement, turning back to face him. 'There's already a layer covering the ground!'

Daniel began to gather her belongings, efficiently placing them in her backpack. 'I know. The storm's coming in from the north. It's already left feet of snow there, and it's gathering force.'

Markie watched absently as he rolled her sleeping-bag into a tight tube and tied it to the frame of her backpack. 'What am I going to do?' she murmured out loud, musing on her options. 'I can't stay here.'

Daniel looked at her incredulously. He might as well have been invisible for all the notice she was taking of him.

'That's why I'm here,' he enunciated slowly. 'I'm taking you back to my house to wait out the storm.'

Markie met his eyes calmly, measuringly. 'I don't think so, thank you.'

'What do you mean, you don't think so?' he exploded incredulously.

'You made it quite clear that I was an intrusion you didn't wish to deal with,' Markie began repressively. 'I, in turn, have no wish to intrude. I can take care of myself.'

Daniel cursed beneath his breath. 'If I hear that statement one more time——' He broke off the threat and drew a steadying breath. Reason. What was called for here was cold, calm reason. 'Have you ever lived in these mountains? Have you ever been here when nature cut loose with a blizzard? People *die*. You'll die unless you find shelter within the next hour!' he finished loudly, ignoring the fact that his reasoning turned out to be neither cold nor calm.

'Well then, if you'll just point me in the right direction——' Markie suggested determinedly.

'That's what I'm doing!' Daniel cursed again. 'Don't you get it? *I'm* the only shelter for miles! There is nothing else.'

'There must be something,' she struggled. 'And abandoned cabin, a cave——'

'Lady, read my lips! There is nothing else. Now let's get out of here.'

With that, Daniel crawled from the protection of the tent and into the deepening snow. Markie stared blankly at the entrance. Well, she had certainly lost that round. If what he said was true, she had no choice. The tent would certainly provide no shelter during a heavy snow-fall; the weight of the snow would cause the lightweight nylon to collapse.

As this thought penetrated her mind, the right flap of the tent was thrown upwards, the whole wall now open to the outdoors. Daniel studied her impatiently from the other side, a tent stake dangling from his fingers.

'If you want to take this thing with you, I suggest you get out here and help me.' His voice was flat.

Markie stared at him, open-mouthed. The snow was falling more heavily now, huge flakes that balanced precariously on every surface. Finally the urgency of the situation became clear to her and she leapt to her feet.

'I'll take the other side,' she told him calmly, surprising him with the competent strength of her tone.

Within minutes they were tearing down the tent and folding it away. There was no time to dry it properly and no time for neatness. In silence they packed away all the belingings Markie had so recently laid out. The warm-up pants and matching sweat-shirt she wore for sleeping would have to suffice for the hike to shelter. There was no time, and no place, to change into jeans.

With one eye to the sky, she tied the final binding on her backpack and lifted the bag.

'Wait!' Daniel's command was brisk and she turned to him questioningly. He reached for her heavy-framed pack and offered his light day pack in its place. 'I'll take your pack; you take mine.'

Markie's mouth firmed determinedly. 'That won't be necessary.'

Daniel sighed in frustration. 'Look, lady——'

'I object to being called "lady",' she interrupted evenly. 'It makes me sound like a poodle. My name is Markie—two syllables, not very complicated. I'm sure if you tried, you could manage to say it.'

'Look, *Markie*,' Daniel began irately, 'this storm is moving in more rapidly than expected.' He made a wide, sweeping gesture to indicate its building intensity. 'In case you haven't noticed, we don't have time for platitudes *or* pride. I'm an experienced hiker——'

'So am I——'

'I'm familiar with the ground we need to cover and I'm a hell of a lot stronger than you,' he continued without pause. 'Now give me your backpack.'

Markie stared at the arrogant hand he held out to her, studying it as if it were something uniquely distasteful. The expression remained in her eyes as she met his gaze. 'It's my backpack.'

The words were simple and direct and without challenge. With four syllables she had conveyed to Daniel her unbending determination. 'Dammit,' he cursed, 'you are the most stubborn, obstreperous——'

'If we don't have time for platitudes,' Markie cut in calmly, 'then I'm sure we don't have time for insults. It's coming down harder.' She stared up into the dark sky and watched the snow glide thickly down. 'How long will it take to get to your house?'

'Normally, thirty minutes,' he answered roughly, still angered by her stubbornness. 'In this. . .that depends on you.'

Her shoulders squared. 'I told you, I'm an experienced——'

'Do a lot of hiking through the mountains during night blizzards, do you?' he mocked.

'Do you?'

He released an aggravated breath. 'I wouldn't be doing it tonight, if it hadn't been for you.'

As far as Markie was concerned, it was an accusation. 'I didn't ask for your help,' she defended angrily, her body stiff. 'I don't need——'

'—anything from me,' he finished for her tightly. 'I know, it's on the record. If it will make you feel better, I'll sign a statement swearing that you didn't ask for help.' He threw his hands up. 'I came here on my own. It's one of my few flaws that I can't let someone die when I know I can save them. A quirk in my personality, I suppose——'

'All right, all right!' Markie surrendered. 'I—appreciate your help,' she managed tightly, dragging the reluctant word from her throat, before pride demanded a rider. 'But I didn't ask for it.'

'You're asking for something,' Daniel warned her tautly before turning away. 'I suggest we get out of here before I give it to you.'

Markie watched him balefully as he shouldered his day pack and scanned the meadow for anything they might have left behind. She had won the battle of the backpack, but she had the uneasy suspicion that the war had only just begun.

With that thought blocking out all others, she focused on him carefully. It was most unsettling to realise that she was beginning something unknown with this man who himself was still, essentially, unknown. She had only her impressions, her feelings, her observations, and her fears to guide her. Before she began the journey, she knew she needed more.

'All right, let's get moving,' Daniel ordered brusquely, leading the way.

He had taken four steps before he realised that Markie was not following. Wearily, he turned to face her, the question on his face not needing voice.

'You haven't even told me your name,' Markie told him quietly.

Daniel studied her in comprehension. He understood the need she could not explain, the demand she could not voice. She was about to follow him through a raging blizzard over unfamiliar ground to an unknown destination. She must need much more from him than his name, but it was all she would ask for. Markie, he was quickly learning, hated to ask for anything.

'My name is Daniel,' he answered just as quietly. 'Daniel Reed.' If she recognised his name, she gave no sign. Daniel observed her minutely and saw—nothing. It was not implausible that she had never heard of him. Perhaps his work simply did not appeal to her. Perhaps her interest was focused in other areas of the field. Perhaps his self-imposed isolation in the mountains, away from the public eye, had finally wrought the miracle he had hoped for and granted him anonymity.

'Daniel,' she repeated softly, causing a strange *frisson* of warmth to touch his skin.

'Two syllables,' he echoed her earlier taunt. 'Not very complicated.'

The name? Markie thought. No, the name was not complicated. But the man was an enigma.

The hike to Daniel's house was a nightmare that Markie would not soon forget. It seemed to be an uphill journey the entire way, and every rock, every patch of grass was coated with a thickening layer of snow that made a mockery of balance.

They had scarcely reached the halfway point when the snowfall thickened ominously. Markie could barely make out Daniel's faint outline a few feet ahead of her. The wind tossed the snow in their faces like so much icy confetti, but it was not a celebration she wanted any part of.

Struggling to keep Daniel in view, she picked up her pace, stepping unwarily on an icy patch of stones. The next thing she knew, she was flat on the ground, stretched out full length as the snow rained down on her. She was exhausted, and considered for the briefest moment just lying there, not moving, and letting the snow fall. It was so quiet and peaceful and she didn't want to fight its calming beauty. . .

'What the hell do you think you're doing?' The incredulous question, growled from a masculine throat, jarred her back to reality.

She turned her head fractionally and made out Daniel's hulking shadow. 'Would you believe, making snow angels?'

He was threateningly silent.

'All right, I slipped,' she gave in tiredly, attempting to push herself up from the ground.

Suddenly, without warning, big hands closed around her, wringing a surprised gasp from her. The feel of those strong hands made her realise suddenly just how long it had been since she had been physically touched by anyone.

Seemingly without effort, Daniel hauled her to her feet and further, bringing her several inches into the air. Their eyes held, even, as Markie's toes dangled over the ground. Daniel read her surprise, felt it in her body, and studied her intently, seeking its source.

'Put me down!'

Daniel blinked. Her tone was as even as a frozen lake, and as cold. Carefully, he lowered her to her feet.

When she came in contact with the ground, Markie immediately felt her feet sliding out from beneath her again. Unwilling to land in an undignified sprawl, she grasped Daniel desperately, her fingers tightening around his muscular forearms. His hands, in turn, tightened automatically around her waist, holding her upright as she regained her balance.

It was then that it hit him—that same overwhelming

feeling of warmth he had experienced when he had first seen her asleep in his wild flowers. It came from her, he registered in confusion. He could feel it flowing from her body and into his at every point of contact. Where his fingers held her, where her hands tightened on his forearms, where their bodies brushed, through heavy-weight clothing, as she struggled for balance. Dear God, it was coming from her!

Markie felt it too. And she was struggling for balance in more than just the physical sense. But the warmth Daniel was generating inside her was hypnotic, as the snow had been hypnotic. If only she could curl up against it and let it soak into every dark and chilly corner of her. . .

It was that thought that brought her up short. No, it could never be like that! She could never let anyone, or anything, into those corners. They must remain out of the light, out of sight, out of pain's way. The warmth he offered wasn't a cure, it was a threat. She had to remember that.

'I'm fine.' The words emerged in a harsh rush from her lips, but she couldn't worry about that now. Pulling from his grip, she instinctively put a foot of distance between them before drawing a calming breath. For the first time she was grateful for the intensity of the snow, because it hid her confusion and unease. 'I'm fine,' she repeated more calmly, avoiding his eyes. 'We can continue now.'

Daniel was doing some adjusting of his own. The cold was seeping back into his flesh, now that she had moved away. He didn't like the sensation one bit. 'Are you hurt?' he asked roughly, denying the emotion.

Markie shook her head in a futile gesture. 'No. Probably just a bruise or two.'

He grimaced. 'That's usually what happens when you fall on your ego.'

She gazed up at him through the driving snow. 'Is that what I fell on?'

'Come on. We have to keep moving.'

'How much further?' she asked, gathering her strength.

Daniel nodded ahead. 'There's a copse of trees up there,' he told her bracingly. 'The house is just on the other side.'

Markie regarded him ironically. 'How do you know there's a copse of trees ahead? All I see is snow.'

'Trust me,' he told her steadily. 'I know my land.'

She nodded. Yes, he would know his land. 'All right, let's go.' She tried to inject a note of calm assurance into her voice, but Daniel heard the hesitation buried beneath.

'I have a rope in my pack,' he told her, eyes measuring. 'We could tie it around ourselves to make sure we didn't get separated.'

Markie received the suggestion in silence. Daniel thought she had no intention of responding until she finally answered in a very, very quiet tone that the wind tried to steal. 'I don't think so, Daniel. I don't work well with any kind of ties.'

In her voice, he heard a note of inescapable, overwhelming truth and self-knowledge that he had no intention of challenging.

'Then let's go,' he urged her, his own words whipped away by the rising wind. 'We're not far from the house now.'

CHAPTER THREE

THE lights of Daniel's house shattered the darkness. Markie couldn't remember a more welcome sight. Now she stumbled on through the stormy night with a purpose, a goal that beckoned.

Daniel threw the back door of the house open and motioned her inside, then followed her into the shelter of his home. Markie found herself in what seemed to be a utility-room. Cupboards, cabinets and counter space comprised three walls. In the corner stood a washer and drier set, and she fumbled briefly with the odd mental picture of Daniel doing laundry.

'Come on, Markie.' She felt a tug on her backpack and then an incredible lightness as it was slipped from her shoulders. 'Get out of your coat and boots and into the kitchen.' Daniel nodded at a door on the fourth wall. 'I have a fire going in there.'

When he turned her around and began unbuttoning her jacket, Markie pulled away, wary of his touch. 'I know how buttons work, thank you,' she dismissed repressively, turning her back on him.

Daniel received that in silence, watching her cold fingers fumble with the buttons. Apparently even the protection of the gloves he had given her hadn't been enough to keep her warm. Odd, when she seemed to generate such heat in him. . .

She heard the sounds of him removing his outer clothes, and the thud of his boots on the tiled floor. Realising that he would only wait for her to finish, she hurried her fingers over the buttons and peeled her jacket off.

'Now the boots,' Daniel ordered expressionlessly, hanging her coat on a nearby hook before she had a chance to do it herself.

Since there was no chair in sight, Markie leaned against the nearest wall and pulled her boots off, one at a time. Once she overbalanced and began tipping towards the floor. She could have sworn she heard a muffled laugh from Daniel, but when she shot him a warning glare he was sober-faced.

Turning away, he threw open the door leading to the kitchen and waved her through. She found herself in a huge room with a large butcher-block table at one end and a plethora of modern appliances at the other. At the corner where the kitchen merged into the formal dining-room next door, a fireplace wrapped around the wall. The lovingly polished hearth stones seemed to reflect the warmth of the flames in the grate.

Markie stared at the fire longingly, frozen, it seemed, from the inside out.

'Why don't you sit on the hearth for a minute?' Daniel suggested, reading her discomfort in the tension of her body. 'I'll make some coffee.'

'I can——' she began instantly, only to be cut off as he pointed imperiously towards the hearth.

'Sit. I'll make the coffee.'

She sat. There seemed to be little point in arguing and less in winning.

Daniel watched from the counter as she absorbed the heat from the fire, shivering with the first onslaught of warmth. She arched unconsciously as the heat penetrated her clothing, and Daniel swallowed and turned away from the sensual response, hers. . .and his.

Markie was totally lost in the pleasure of warmth once

again seeping into her body, and so didn't hear him move as he crossed the room to her side, coffee-cup in hand.

'Careful,' he warned, handing her the cup.

She met his eyes and nodded silently. She traced the pattern of the fire's glow as it bathed his skin and watched his throat work with his first swallow of the coffee.

He was handsome, she discovered in some surprise. Their encounters up to this point had left her with neither the time nor the inclination to study him on a physical level, because she had been so overwhelmed by him in an altogether different way.

His hair was dark brown and a little rough at the collar. A strong, natural wave saved him from looking unkempt. Instead, his hair appeared tousled, as if he had just run an impatient hand through the dark waves. Against his tanned skin, the steel-grey eyes were uncanny, unexpected. She imagined they would change from dove to slate with strong emotion, but now they were the colour of a rainy Sunday, and totally impenetrable. He was several inches over six feet, with the broad shoulders and trim hips that spoke of a man in superior physical condition.

And why not? Markie questioned herself silently. He apparently lived here in the middle of nowhere. There would be ample opportunity, maybe necessity, for physical exertion. Extensive hiking was doubtless responsible for the hardness of those long, masculine legs encased in snug blue jeans. Chopping wood for the fire would have developed the muscular toughness of his upper torso. The hard, tanned angles of face and jaw indicated long days spent in the sun and the wind. And his hands. . .Markie's gaze moved to the coffee-cup where one long-fingered hand curved around the stoneware, seeking warmth, and she gasped soundlessly. Good lord, his hands were beautiful! Strong and lean and somehow gentle-looking, with long, artistic fingers that seemed made to hold a paintbrush or a musical instrument. Yet they were tanned as well, and Markie knew the palms would be roughened from physical labour.

It was perhaps the strength of his features that fascinated her the most. There was no compromise in the slashing cheekbones, no forgiveness in the long mouth, no softness in the stubborn jaw. There was no softness *anywhere* in Daniel Reed, she assessed finally. Not in his face or his form, not even in those beautiful, beckoning hands.

So why wasn't she afraid?

Daniel knew she was staring, but considered it only fair. He felt as if he had been staring at her since their meeting that afternoon. She was beautiful, but he had known and accepted that from the first glance. Her beauty was not the perfection of cold plastic conforming to a mould. It wasn't that easy; nothing about Markie was. From her head to her toes, she was a vibrant, glorious demand—as sharp as a razor's edge and as subtle as a spring breeze. Her hair was the colour of shadows, hinting at secrets and passion. Against her ivory skin, it had the impact of barren branches caressed by snow. Emerald-green eyes flared with challenge and laughter and mystery within her delicate face. In his thirty-four years, Daniel had met many beautiful women, but they had not commanded this incredible need he was fighting to dig beneath Markie's surface and find what lay hidden. Her mind, her heart, her needs. . .

'Drink your coffee,' he told her brusquely, pushing that provocative thought away. 'It's getting cold.'

Markie brought the cup to her lips. 'I was just enjoying

the fire,' she excused, taking a sip and grimacing horribly.

'You don't like coffee?' he hazarded, gauging her reaction.

She swallowed with difficulty. 'Coffee? Oh—er—the coffee's fine.' She speculated on whether a cup of tea might be an improvement, then decided not to risk it.

'I guess I made it a little strong,' he began, restraining his humour at her polite remonstrations.

'No,' Markie assured him hurriedly as she took another sip. 'It's very—filling.'

Daniel's mouth twitched suspiciously, but his cup blocked the smile from view. 'I've never heard coffee referred to that way. You must be hungry.'

'No!' she denied hastily, unwilling to fall more deeply into his debt. 'I—ate before I went to sleep.'

Daniel nodded his understanding, and an awkward silence settled between them. Outside the only noise to be heard was the wailing wind as it whipped the snow into incredible drifts. Inside there was no dripping tap, no drifting music, only the sound of the logs crackling with flames.

When Markie could stand it no longer, she asked a question of major concern. 'Do you live here. . .alone?'

He studied her ironically. He didn't think he had ever heard such dread instilled in a single question. 'Yes. All alone.'

Markie sighed. 'Do you know how long this storm is going to keep up?'

He shrugged. 'It's a major spring blizzard. Parts of northern Colorado are buried under three feet and more of snow, and it's going to dump more here. And even after it stops. . .'

Her head shot up at his warning tone. 'Even after it stops. . .?' she prompted.

Daniel rubbed his temple distractedly. 'Well, think about it, Markie! We're on top of a mountain that's privately owned, with no public roads or maintenance.'

'You said you only owned part of it,' she protested, reminding him of their first encounter.

He quickly dashed her hopes. 'What I don't own is part of a National Forest—untouched and inaccessible. I lease it from the government.'

'So, in effect, the whole mountain is yours.'

'In effect,' he conceded drily.

She regarded him in stunned amazement. 'What do you do all winter?'

Daniel smiled grimly. 'I live in solitude, from the first snow until the spring thaw.'

'But if there's an emergency——?' she tried dazedly.

'I have a radio,' he shrugged. 'In an emergency I could radio out for a chopper to pick me up.'

'What about food, electricity, phone service——?'

'I stock up on supplies every spring and autumn, there's a generator outside, and who needs a phone?' His tone was casual to the point of carelessness.

'You don't have a phone?' Markie was trying to take it all in. Once again she looked around the comfortable kitchen, noting its bright, clean appearance and modern appliances. 'You don't strike me as a hermit.'

Daniel issued an unwilling laugh. God, if only she knew! 'I'm not a hermit. I don't shun human contact. It's simply that circumstances dictate that for six months or so out of the year, I'm pretty much isolated.'

'Circumstances that you arranged,' Markie pointed out carefully.

He studied her in silence. 'Circumstances that I don't fight against.'

'And what do you do while you're all alone up here,

Daniel?' she asked, intensely curious about how he lived
his life.

'What do you do when you're all alone on a hiking
trip?' he countered evenly.

Markie thought of her work and said nothing. When
it became apparent that she wasn't going to answer him,
Daniel gestured to her cup. 'More coffee?'

'No!' she declined in self-protection. 'I'm—er—trying
to cut down.'

'Smart move,' he commented, crossing the room to
refill his own cup. 'The guest bedroom is over there.' He
used his cup to point to a hallway that led from the
dining-room. 'You might as well get comfortable.'

Markie wasn't even given time to protest.

'If you want to use the laundry facilities, that's fine. I
don't imagine that four days on the trail has left you with
much to wear.' His eyes were steady and calm.

'I don't want to put you out,' she began quickly. 'I
could just wait out the storm——'

'For days?' Daniel challenged. 'And then what? Call a
helicopter to come and pick you up? I'm afraid in the
midst of a spring blizzard, you wouldn't rate as an
emergency.'

Markie thought of the campers and hikers who might
have been caught unaware by the freak storm, people
trapped outside in its fury. And she thought of the
position she would have been in, had it not been for
Daniel Reed. She hadn't even thanked him for saving
her life, for that, surely, was what he had done.

'You're right,' she told him softly. 'I—haven't even
thanked you for coming for me. I would have been
trapped out there, unprotected.'

He evaded her gratitude neatly. 'But you're not.
You're here in a warm, dry place and safe from the
storm.' His face shadowed suddenly. 'I didn't even

think. Is there someone you need to get a message to? Someone who'll worry when you don't show up?'

'No.'

Daniel regarded her narrowly. 'We can relay a message with the radio——'

'Mr Reed,' she broke in gently, 'there's no one.'

'What about the rangers at the park headquarters? Surely you checked in with them before you began your trip?'

Markie dropped her eyes guiltily. 'Well, actually. . .'

'You didn't check in,' he muttered, disbelieving, running a distracted hand through his dark hair. 'What kind of stupid, irresponsible stunt was that?'

Her chin tilted defensively. 'I hadn't planned on being gone so long. It was just an. . .impulse. Besides, I can——'

'Don't you say it,' Daniel interrupted with dangerous softness. 'Don't you dare say it!' He measured her defiant expression and sighed roughly. 'Why don't you go take a hot shower to drive the cold away? Coffee obviously wasn't the answer.'

She met his gaze in indecision. To stay meant becoming beholden to him, but she was already that. And beholden on a very basic level. She owed him her life. To leave was. . .impossible; the storm's fury was increasing instead of levelling off. To do nothing would be stupid. Daniel didn't need a useless ornament on his hearth. Squaring her shoulders, Markie accepted the weight of her debt. Somehow, some way she would have to repay it.

Daniel watched her stiffen and sighed. 'If I promise not to do the one thing you seem to hate more than anything else, would you go and take your shower?'

Markie tilted her head questioningly. 'What's that?'

'I won't offer to help.'

She received that ironic promise without comment. She deserved the verbal slap, she supposed. But if she were going to stay with Daniel—and it looked as if she had no choice—she couldn't stay like this.

Bracing herself mentally, she prepared to issue her proposal. 'Mr Reed——'

'Daniel,' he corrected instantly. 'You can't be formal with a man who can't return the favour.' Meeting her puzzled glance, he reminded her, 'You didn't tell me your last name.'

'It's Smith,' she supplied.

'Smith?'

'You have a problem with that?'

Daniel shrugged. 'It's a pretty common name.'

'And?' she challenged defensively.

'It doesn't suit,' he answered simply.

Markie blinked, uncertain if he had really meant to compliment her. 'It's better than none,' she dismissed finally, memories causing her hands to tighten into fists at her side. 'But you can call me whatever you want. I'll answer. . .or I won't. Try Bubba or "hey, you" or——'

'Markie?'

She drew a deep breath and threw him a sheepish smile, regretting her tirade. In the long run, it mattered not at all. 'Yeah. Markie's fine.'

'Now that,' Daniel considered, 'is a very unusual name. What's it short for?'

She ignored him completely. 'Daniel, I've been here for less than thirty minutes and I'm tired of being your guest.'

His eyes narrowed threateningly. 'If you think you're going back out into that blizzard——'

'No. No, that's not what I meant,' she denied quickly. 'And I didn't mean to sound. . .ungrateful. It's just——' she bit her lip in frustration. 'I'm not good at this! I'm uncomfortable being trapped here, intruding on your privacy.'

'I brought you here, remember. No one forced me.'

'Please! You made your feelings on the subject quite clear to me in the meadow. And now I'm committing an even more grievous trespass.' She grimaced. 'Maybe you really should see about that fence, Daniel.'

His face lost all expression. 'Even fences don't keep out the wild flowers, Markie.'

'But I'm not a wild flower.'

'Aren't you?' His jaw tightened before he turned away. 'So you don't want to be my guest and you can't leave. What's left?'

Markie peeped at him hopefully. 'A gentlemen's agreement?'

Daniel's mouth quirked wryly. 'One, and possibly both of us, fail to qualify for the title.'

'Metaphorically speaking,' Markie amended.

'Of course.'

'If you don't expect me to act like your guest,' she rushed on, ignoring his dry tone, 'I won't expect you to act like my host.'

Daniel considered the proposal in thoughtful silence for several seconds before demanding, 'What the hell does that mean?'

'It means that I'll go crazy if I have to spend another thirty minutes this way,' Markie exploded quietly, her eyes underlining her frustration. 'Searching for polite conversation to bridge the uneasy silences. Doing nothing while you provide and——'

'——accepting my help with anything,' Daniel finished in disgust, cutting to the real heart of her discomfort. 'Even something as trivial as a lousy cup of coffee!'

'I don't consider saving my life as trivial,' Markie

corrected, her eyes turning throughtful. 'But it *was* a lousy cup of coffee.'

'It was a little strong,' he defended grudgingly. 'But it was hot, and that's what you needed——'

'Daniel, please!' Markie drew his attention. 'All I'm saying is that we got off to a bad start. I can't be snowbound with a rival for days on end. Can't we get past the hostility and move up to being——?'

'Strangers?' Daniel suggested, his gaze cutting.

Markie searched his face. Unconsciously giving voice to thought, she whispered, 'How odd.'

'Odd?'

'I never thought of you as a stranger,' she answered simply.

He struggled with that piece of whimsy for several long seconds. 'You worry me, Markie Smith. You really do.'

'When I worry *me* I'll take action. Until then,' Markie grinned and held out her hand, 'temporary friends?'

Daniel studied her offered hand warily, remembering the intense physical reaction she sparked in him. Unwilling to take the risk, he shook his head. 'Temporary strangers, Markie.'

Markie most definitely noted the distinction.

The shower was eminently satisfying. After four days of off-trail hiking and making do with quick baths in nearby streams of ice-cold water, soap and steamy water were a sensual experience. Every glorious moment helped fade the memory of the forced, frozen march through the snow.

Donning Daniel's blue and white striped shirt brought it all back again. He had left it for her while she showered, and Markie measured her appearance ironically. Daniel's dress shirt reached halfway down her thighs, falling straight and shapeless from the broad shoulder seams that rested near her elbows.

The many faces of fashion, she thought wryly, laughing at herself. She missed entirely the intense emphasis that the masculine garment brought to her feminine form. The difference in fit, from shoulder to thigh, was a subtle reminder of the difference in gender.

Markie towel-dried her hair as best she could and let it brush the line of her jaw in a tangled mop. Hardly the picture of glamour, she thought ironically. But then she wasn't trying to impress anyone. Was she?

In an effort to escape from the question she left the bedroom. She was drawn back to the kitchen by the remembered warmth of the fire and the tempting aroma of cooking food.

Daniel was at the stove, stirring something in a pan. Markie watched him from the doorway for a moment, struck by the ease of his movements. He was, she decided, a multi-faceted individual. She had barely scratched the surface of what he was, with the little that she knew about him.

She followed his intense gaze through the window, where outside the snow pounded down in a thick white wall. Daniel tightened his jaw grimly, muttering beneath his breath, 'Snowbound.'

Markie cleared her throat softly, deciding to announce her presence before she was privy to any further grim pronouncements.

To his credit, Daniel did not whirl around in embarrassment or accusation. His back stiffened just a bit, but he continued to stir the contents of the pan on the stove.

'Find everything you need?' he asked laconically.

Markie moved into the room. 'Yes, thank you. The hot water was wonderful.'

'Good. I'm heating up some beef stew,' he announced

decisively, turning to fix a commanding gaze on her. 'And you're going to eat it——'

The words halted abruptly as Daniel's eyes settled on her. His face went curiously blank as his gaze moved from the damp, tangled hair to the pure vulnerability in her face. When his eyes dropped to her slender body, lost in the oversized shirt, Markie shifted uncomfortably.

'It's a bit big,' she noted inanely, lifting her hands to show him the four inches of sleeve dangling beyond her fingertips.

Daniel's gaze made a reluctant return from her bare, shapely legs. Their eyes held briefly before his snapped away. 'You need a robe,' he muttered abruptly, already striding past her. 'I should have thought of it—before.'

'Thank you,' she managed faintly, addressing his back.

He stopped and turned to face her. 'Do you really have a blue belt in Tae Kwondo, Markie?'

Her smile lasted for perhaps a quarter of a second. 'What do you think?'

Daniel shook his head. 'I think I'd better go get that robe.'

Markie watched him leave the room with thoughtful eyes, then drifted towards the stove to stir the stew. The thick gravy bubbled gently, rising steam filling the kitchen with a heavenly aroma. With typical decisiveness, she turned down the flame beneath the pan and pushed up her sleeves. Biscuits would go nicely with the meal.

She was opening the overhead cabinet, looking for the necessary ingredients, when Daniel returned. He watched as his shirt slipped dramatically up the back of her legs, caressing the sweet curve of her thighs and higher.

'What are you doing?'

Markie didn't bother to turn as she answered absently, 'Looking for flour.'

Daniel stared at her blankly. 'Flour?'

She moved to the next cabinet. 'Um. And baking powder and salt and shortening and milk and butter.'

Daniel mentally recited the list of ingredients and came up with the right answer. 'Biscuits?'

'Right.' She flashed him a smile. 'I make the best biscuits east of the Rockies.'

'We're *in* the Rockies,' he pointed out gravely.

Her smiled deflated. 'Oh. Yeah.' She eyed him cautiously. 'Maybe we're in trouble.'

Daniel laughed softly and handed her the dark blue robe in his hands. While she slipped into the voluminous garment, he moved to the pantry to gather her ingredients. 'Milk and butter in the refrigerator, Markie,' he called over his shoulder as he moved to the table, arms full.

Markie retrieved the necessary items from the refrigerator while Daniel located a bowl and measuring cups. Finally, with everything at hand, she quickly set about mixing the biscuit dough. Daniel sat at the table and watched as the sleeves from the robe slipped down time and again, until the cuffs were white with flour.

'Darn it!' Markie grumbled, pushing the sleeves up for the twentieth time.

Daniel grabbed one cuff and hauled her towards him, pulling until she was positioned in front of him, between his parted knees.

'What are you——?'

He calmly and efficiently rolled the sleeve of the robe up her slender arm, then set to work on the shirt-sleeve beneath. Her flour-dusted hands dangled near his shoulders, and Daniel was very conscious of their slender warmth. When he started on the other sleeve, Markie seemed compelled to protest.

'Daniel. . .'

He shook his head. 'Don't tell me; let me guess. You know how sleeves work.' His mocking words were a reminder of her earlier refusal of his help with her jacket.

'Yes.'

He finished the sleeve and dropped his hands. 'And I know how to make biscuits.'

Markie tilted her head. 'So this is a pay-back?'

'Pay-back?'

'To make us even,' she explained.

Daniel sighed. 'If that's what you want, Markie.'

She nodded. 'But then I still owe you for the stew and the shower and the shirt and the robe and the fire and. . .the rescue.'

He met her eyes. 'I don't take cash or travellers' cheques or credit cards.'

'So I'll pay you back in kind.' Markie's chin rose determinedly.

'In kind?' Daniel's eyes gleamed with interest.

Markie ignored him easily. 'I'll make dinner for you.'

'You don't have a kitchen.'

She raised imperious brows. 'I meant here.'

'Are you going to loan me a shirt and robe too?' Daniel queried innocently.

She bit her lip in vexation.

'And what about the shower?' he pressed on. 'How are you going to pay me back for that? Scrub my back?'

She didn't even hear the suggestiveness in that; she was occupied with another aspect of her repayment plan. 'And the rescue,' she mused worriedly. 'I can never pay you back for the rescue.'

Daniel's eyes were suddenly darkly shadowed and aware. Swiftly he rose to his feet, almost toppling her in the process. 'I don't want any "pay-back" from you, Markie. It's not a game I play.'

'Game!' she repeated, her brow creasing in confusion. 'It's not a game, Daniel; it's life. Anything you want in this world, anything you achieve, you pay for. You can't deny that.'

He held her still with his eyes. 'Anything, Markie? What about wild flowers?'

'You bought them,' she reminded him quietly. 'With the most common payment of all: green paper and metal coins.'

'And dreams?'

She shrugged. 'We pay for those by believing in reality.'

'And love?' he pressed. 'Do we pay for love as well?'

Markie's face became shuttered. 'How can you even ask?'

Daniel's gaze sharpened, but he answered simply, 'I've never been in love.'

'Neither have I.' She turned away. 'Maybe it's because neither of us is willing to pay the price.'

With great deliberation, she moved back to the biscuit dough. She quickly completed the task of cutting out the rounds and placing them on a baking sheet Daniel provided.

'It should take about ten minutes,' she promised, separating herself neatly from their earlier discussion. 'If you'll show me where the plates are, I'll set the table.'

For a moment, Daniel looked as if he were going to argue with her, and force the conversation back to the original subject. But one look at Markie's blank, determined face changed his mind. Silently he moved to the cabinet that housed the china and handed two plates down to her.

While she set the table with napkins and cutlery, he

kept watch over the biscuits. When they were golden brown he took them from the oven and transferred them to a small bread basket. Markie ladled the stew into a large serving dish and placed it on the table next to the biscuits. They worked well together, co-ordinating responsibilities without any conversation at all.

When everything was in place, they sat at the table and began. The stew was as heavenly as it smelled, thick with chunks of meat and vegetables.

'Fresh vegetables,' Markie noted suspiciously. 'I thought you said you were isolated up here.'

He regarded her drily. 'I took advantage of the weather and drove into town yesterday—I was craving anything that wasn't frozen or canned. We won't starve.'

Markie concentrated on her meal, slightly ashamed of her unspoken accusation. 'The stew is delicious,' she complimented him appeasingly. 'Did you make it from scratch?'

Daniel smiled over a fluffy biscuit dripping with butter. 'One of my minor talents.'

She tapped one knuckle lightly. 'The hands of a chef.'

'The stomach of a glutton,' he corrected easily. 'I couldn't very well eat frozen dinners for six months straight.'

Markie sobered, his comment bringing her situation into sharp focus. Suddenly she was again aware of the wind howling ceaselessly and the frozen chill of silent snow steadily piling up outside. She was trapped by circumstances beyond her control, trapped again. . . She shivered reflexively.

'You're chilled,' said Daniel, witnessing the shiver. 'You shouldn't be sitting here with damp hair.'

'I'm OK,' she dismissed, avoiding his eyes.

But Daniel was already picking up their plates and

moving them to the hearth, motioning her to sit before the softly glowing flames. 'Your hair will dry faster here.'

Markie gave in gracefully, arranging the long robe around her with a grimace. 'My hair is so thick, it usually takes a long time for it to dry.'

Daniel's eyes were fixed on her wavy locks. 'It's very——'

'Black,' Markie finished disgustedly. 'Like mud.'

He reacted instantly to the dismissive tone. Like shadows on the snow,' he corrected quietly. 'Dark fire.'

Markie studied his face in unwilling fascination. 'That was—poetic.'

His mouth twisting with self-derision, Daniel pulled back. 'Sorry. This is what living alone does for you.'

'I liked it.'

He shrugged uneasily and concentrated on his stew.

Markie sighed and moved to another topic. 'Did you have this house built or did you just happen into the perfect place?'

'Perfect place?' One eye brow rose in query.

'Well, sure,' she explained. 'This is your perfect place, isn't it? It's where you belong?'

Daniel's expression was thoughtful. 'I suppose so. . .'

'I bet you had the house built,' she hazarded confidently.

'Six years ago,' he conceded. 'I even drew up the first plans by myself. I knew exactly what I wanted.'

Markie nodded. She had known that from the instant she opened her eyes in the meadow that afternoon. She looked around, taking in the obvious signs of comfort and convenience.

'Funny, when you said you were taking me to your house to shelter from the storm, I somehow pictured a tiny log cabin tucked in the woods, like Abraham Lincoln's home.'

'You've been to see it?'

She nodded absently. 'Sure.'

'You've been a lot of places,' he hazarded.

'I travel a lot.'

He was silent for a moment, then he fired the next salvo. 'Where do you live?'

Markie met his challenge calmly. 'I live where I am.'

'Another aspect of your "practical" life?' he mocked.

'You do seem to be having trouble with the concept, Daniel,' she conceded quietly. 'But I could hardly live where I'm not, could I?'

'Why not?' he returned cynically, eyes shadowed. 'Most of us do.'

Markie studied him carefully, unsure how to respond. As it turned out, there was no need, because Daniel was challenging her again.

'Did it ever occur to you, Markie, that the answers in your "practical" life are just too damn simple? I live where I am,' he mimicked roughly. 'I stay until I leave. What are you going to do when those answers don't work any more?'

'Look for new ones,' she answered quietly, confused by his driven tone. 'If the situation arises.'

His mouth twisted. 'It will.'

'You seem sure.'

'I am sure. The "situation" is life. If there are answers, they aren't easy.'

'Does it occur to you,' she challenged in return, 'that your answers are too complicated? That when everything seems to fall into the realm of grey, the only answer is to search for the colours?'

Their eyes held in silence, measuring.

'No,' Daniel answered at length, turning away. 'It never occurs to me.'

Markie put her plate on the stones beside her, disturbed by the conversation. It wasn't her place to judge the way Daniel lived, nor to answer to him about her chosen lifestyle. Temporary strangers didn't probe too deeply.

'My hair is almost dry,' she said into the silence that had fallen. 'I think I'll go to bed now.'

Daniel nodded, picking up both plates and carrying them to the sink. 'You've had a rough day.'

'And you,' she added, rising to her feet. 'I'll help clean up.'

'It's done,' he told her, loading the plates in the dishwasher. 'Go to bed.'

Markie hesitated, but Daniel didn't turn. His stiff back seemed to be silently reinforcing his order.

'All right,' she sighed, taking reluctant steps to the doorway before stopping. 'Daniel, thank you for saving me from facing the storm alone.'

'You're welcome.' His voice was like a feather brushing her skin. 'Go to bed.'

Markie went.

CHAPTER FOUR

MARKIE awoke early the next morning to smothering silence. For a moment she lay without moving, perfectly aware of where she was and how she had got there. The sudden storm, the forced march to Daniel's house; it was all very clear in her mind.

Daniel was very clear in her mind. For such a private man, his actions of the day before surpised her. He appeared to cherish the solitude of this mountain fortress he called home, yet he had not hesitated to come after her when danger threatened. Obviously there was much more to Daniel Reed than the somewhat aloof façade he had presented upon their first meeting. She wondered suddenly how much of those depths she would have the opportunity to explore. How much she could afford to explore. . .

That tantalising question was enough to chase Markie out of bed. In an effort to redirect her wandering thoughts, she threw the covers aside. Again she wondered at the curious silence of the room, and crossed to the window to investigate. Pushing the curtain aside, she stared in stunned disbelief.

A white-blanketed world greeted her from the other side of the window, shadowed still by continuing snowfall. The violence of the storm had lessened, and the wind had died down, but flakes still fell steadily from the leaden sky. And though the fury of the night before had gone, it had left behind at least two feet of thick, treacherous snow.

No wonder it was so quiet, Markie thought in amazement. The blankets of snow deadened every sound. Any living thing possessing a modicum of sense had to be burrowed deep in a warm, safe shelter, waiting for the thaw. As she was. . .

She let the curtain drop into place and turned to survey the room. Last night she had been too tired, too distracted by the unexpected events of the day to take much notice of her surroundings. Now she studied them with interest.

It was, quite obviously, a guest bedroom. It was also, quite obviously, seldom if ever used. The colour scheme of cream and slate was attractive and totally impersonal. There was no hint of personality in the room, no stamp of ownership. It was a shell that hosted no occupant, no memory of an occupant. So unlike the rest of Daniel's house, Markie mused curiously, remembering the welcoming kitchen and the glimpse she had caught of the intimate living area. It was obviously the vitality of Daniel's presence that had brought them life. She was suddenly, overwhelmingly curious to see the rest of his house, to find more of Daniel Reed.

She was heading for the shower when she noticed the pile of clothes neatly folded on the chair. It was part of a small sitting area at the opposite end of the room. She studied the pile, easily recognising the clothing she had left in her backpack upon entering the house and the warm-ups she had worn for the hike. Last night she had completely forgotten Daniel's offer of laundry facilities. Apparently he had not. He must have washed them after she had retired for the night and brought them in while she slept. Two pairs of jeans, three shirts, her warm-ups, and every pair of gaily coloured panties she had brought along were neatly folded and spotlessly clean. Markie thought of those beautiful hands touching her most intimate apparel and felt a curious ache begin in some deep and unfamiliar part of her.

Flushing, she turned away, searching for distraction. A brisk shower, she thought determinedly, grabbing her toiletries from the backpack propped against the chair before heading towards the connecting bathroom once again. A brisk shower, and then—Daniel.

She brushed her teeth, showered and combed the tangles from her damp hair without once ever looking at herself in the mirror. Her face, she thought not for the first time, was depressingly expressive. At the moment, she wasn't ready to deal with what it would reveal.

After absently pulling on jeans and a shirt, she left the bedroom to wind her way through the silent house. In the kitchen she found a fire glowing softly in the hearth and an echoing stillness. Other than a fresh pot of steaming coffee, there was no sign of Daniel. Markie surveyed the room carefully, looking for an indication that he had had breakfast before he disappeared. Finding none, she rolled up her sleeves decisively. She would make breakfast for them both, and if Daniel was anywhere nearby, the smell of bacon and coffee would surely draw him out.

Markie felt momentarily uneasy as she searched the refrigerator, then sensibly brushed the discomfort aside. She had to eat, it was a simple as that. The only thing worse than making free with Daniel's food and making breakfast for them both was sitting here and waiting for Daniel to do it for her.

She had just given the bacon one final turn when the utility-room door opened and he swept in with a wave of bracing cold. His face was flushed with the frigid morning air and a light dusting of snow whitened his dark hair. Unwillingly, Markie studied him more closely, drawn in by the vitality that was so much a part of him.

He had obviously left his coat and boots in the utility-room, because he was in shirt-sleeves and stockinged feet. In some strange way, it made him seem vulnerable. Markie forced the thought away. There was very little vulnerability in Daniel Reed, she reminded herself. He had made that abundantly clear in the short time they had been together. Although it was barely seven o'clock in the morning, he looked as if he had been awake for hours, his grey eyes sharp and alert.

It was the sharpness of those eyes that brought her bumping back to reality. While she had been unashamedly studying him, Daniel had been returning the favour. She felt his gaze move over her entire body, from her own stockinged feet to her drying tumble of hair. For some unknown reason, his eyes kicked to life that little ache she was trying so hard to ignore.

'Good morning,' he said quietly, breaking free of the stillness between them and closing the door behind him.

'Good morning,' Markie returned, busying herself at the stove. 'It sure is cold out there.' She could have kicked herself for the inane comment when she saw Daniel's mouth quirk.

But he didn't call her on it. 'Yes, it is,' he agreed easily, peering over her shoulder at the sizzling bacon. 'Bacon smells good.'

The tension in her back eased just a bit. 'I made enough for both of us. I hope you haven't eaten yet.'

'Not yet,' he concurred.

Markie busied herself laying the bacon on a paper towel. 'How do you like your eggs?' she queried.

'Over easy.'

She nodded and began to break the eggs into the skillet. Daniel shifted beside her, reaching for the plates in the cabinet to the right. His hard shoulder, clad in the chambray shirt, brushed against her ear, and she pulled away nervously.

'Sorry,' he apologised succinctly, turning to set the table.

Markie stared into the skillet in dismay. She had to overcome this. . .awareness of Daniel. They were going to be stranded together until the snow cleared. It would be hard enough for two people who were accustomed to living their lives very much alone without the added pressure of this—attraction.

'Er—Daniel?'

He didn't even look up. 'Yes?'

'How do you feel about scrambled eggs?'

Daniel flashed her a smile. 'Some of my best friends are scrambled eggs.'

Markie gave an easy laugh. 'Toast?'

'It's made.' His brief answer caused her to look to where he had just pushed down the lever on the toaster. Again, she thought how well they seemed to work together.

After scooping the eggs on to a serving dish, she carried it and the platter of bacon to the table. Daniel followed with the toast and they both sat.

'You were out early,' she remarked, cutting her toast in half.

He swallowed a bite of bacon before answering. 'I went to check on the generator.'

'Generator?'

'Um,' he agreed. 'It's the only power source for the house.'

Her brow wrinkled. 'That must be some generator.'

He shrugged. 'Mainly it provides for the lights and appliances. The house is heated with the wood stove in the living area and the solar panels on the roof.'

'And the fireplaces,' she added meticulously.

'They're warm enough if you're right in front of them,' Daniel allowed. 'And mine are better designed to distribute heat than most. But a fireplace is generally a poor source for practical heating.'

'Then why did you bother?' She tilted her head interestedly.

'I like the look of them,' he answered simply. 'I like the sound of the flames on the logs and the scent of comfort and. . .home.'

Markie nodded, eyes thoughtful. If there was one thing she understood, it was the need for home, whether it was illusion or reality. When she left here, she would take with her a few new ideas for her own home. Fireplaces and—when she left here. . . Her eyes moved to the window over the sink. 'It's still snowing.'

Daniel measured her tone. 'Not like last night.'

'But enough to worry about.'

'The weather service says we can expect another six to eight inches before it stops,' he told her frankly. 'By tomorrow morning we should have clear skies.'

'And three feet of snow,' Markie whispered, appalled at the thought of so much snow. 'Oh, Daniel! What about the wild flowers?'

'Markie,' he soothed, touched by the distress in her voice, 'I told you, wild flowers are tough. Just as some take root in rock, some flourish even in the snow. Their beauty's not as fragile as you think.'

'No,' she agreed thoughtfully, so quietly that he had to strain to hear. 'I guess true beauty never is.'

Daniel watched as she seemed to deliberately shake herself free of her thoughts and met his eyes. There were no secrets there now, he thought.

'Finished?'

He looked down blankly at his empty plate, truly unaware that he had eaten his breakfast. 'Finished.'

He stood and began clearing the dishes, allowing Markie to help without comment.

'Daniel——' she began hesitantly as he rinsed their plates.

'Hmm?'

'Thank you for washing my clothes. I forgot all about them last night.'

'You're welcome,' he told her evenly, wondering what colour of silky panties she was wearing beneath those tight jeans.

'You didn't have to do it,' she felt obliged to add.

Daniel thought of her long, smooth legs and tempting thighs peeping out from beneath the hem of his shirt and laughed in self-derision. 'I think I did.'

'I don't——' Markie began confusedly, only to be interrupted by his determined question.

'Do you have any plans for today?'

'No,' she managed, somewhat bemused by his actions. 'I guess scuba diving is out.'

He smiled unwillingly. 'How about a tour of the house?'

She perked up. 'I'd like that.'

Daniel put the skillet away and dried his hands. 'Let's go, then.' He threw the towel on to the counter and gestured easily. 'This is the kitchen.'

'No!' Markie pretended amazement.

'Yes,' he insisted, deadpan. 'The refrigerator is a dead giveaway.'

She followed as he rounded the corner to the foraml dining-room. 'I take my meals in the kitchen,' he told her. 'But it seemed like a good idea to include a dining-room, just in case. Besides, I like to work here sometimes.'

'Work?' Markie repeated quietly, testing just how far he would go.

Daniel blinked and turned away. 'Yes. The guest
bedroom and my room are down this hallway,' he
motioned to their right. 'Both have private bathrooms.'
He didn't offer to show her his room and she didn't
press the issue. The double doors leading into his room
were set further down the hallway and on the opposite
side from her own. She hadn't noticed them last night.

'You must have been very quiet leaving your room
this morning,' she commented idly. 'Or you left very
early. I didn't hear a thing.'

He shrugged. 'There's a door leading outside to the
patio,' he dismissed, not bothering to tell her that he
hadn't spent the night in his room, that he had spent the
long dark hours upstairs, trying to understand the
unfamiliar emotions she roused in him.

For all the good it had done him, he mocked silently.
At first light he had still been as confused and reluctant,
as determined and uneasy. The generator had been an
excuse to leave the house, but Markie had been the
reason. Markie, snuggled under the down quilt in his
guest bedroom, with his shirt sliding off one smooth
white shoulder. He had gone in around midnight to leave
her clothes and she had been deeply asleep, unaware of
his presence. But he had been. . .aware of her.

Now, as then, he turned away abruptly, searching for
breathing space. 'The living area is through here.'

He moved, and Markie followed.

The living area was large, running the entire length of
the house. Despite its size, it radiated a certain intimacy,
with furniture clustered in several conversation areas. In
front of the efficient wood-burning stove was a comfortable overstuffed sofa in forest-green. It was flanked by a
multi-hued lounger that looked invitingly soft. Some
distance away, ensconced before a wall of floor-to-ceiling

bookcases, were two plush chairs. The walls were a soothing cream, broken occasionally by framed prints. Several area rugs decorated the gleaming hardwood floor, adding a touch of warmth and comfort.

A breakfast bar separated the living area from the kitchen, which was hidden behind a series of shutters. There was a large bay window with a seat overlooking a snow-shrouded panorama. The front door was flanked with leaded glass. The ceiling was cathedral, with a skylight bringing in an unexpected source of light. Twenty-five feet of open space between the ceiling and the floor added a sense of openness. A huge half-loft ran the length of the back of the house, with stairs leading up from near the front door.

Markie's appraisal was deeply appreciative. 'It's beautiful.'

'It's what I wanted,' Daniel rejoined, a trace of pride and something else in his tone.

'A fortress?'

He shook his head. 'A home, Markie. I guess you wouldn't understand that.'

She took immediate offence. 'What do you mean, I wouldn't understand that?'

He eyed her warily, wondering at her defensive posture. 'You told me that you travel quite a bit. And that tent of yours looks pretty well used.'

'It is. And I—do,' she admitted, then subsided into silence.

'I used to travel,' he said abruptly, breaking into the silence.

'Did you?'

He turned away, pushing his hands into his pockets. 'That was before I decided that I needed this more.'

'How did you——?'

'There are plenty of books to read,' he broke in briskly, pulling away from the strange and fragile air between them, and away from her question. 'I lean more towards biographies and mysteries, but there are all types.'

'What's upstairs?' The simple question fell into weighted silence.

Finally, Daniel answered reluctantly, 'The music-room.'

Markie's eyes brightened. 'Music-room? Really? Does it have a piano?'

He read the eagerness in her eyes and smiled indulgently. 'Yes, it has a piano.' Against his better judgement, against all instincts for privacy and self-preservation that had developed in him over the years, he asked, 'Want to see it?'

Markie nodded enthusiastically and followed him to the stairs. She was on the last step when she stopped abruptly, captured by the simple beauty of the room. Daniel turned to watch her face, closely monitoring the expressions that chased across her features. He saw pleasure and delight as she studied the entire back wall of glass that opened the loft to the outdoors. Through the snow, it was impossible to see beyond the balcony, but jagged mountains rose forever in the distance. The brightness of the blanketing snow was blinding, covering everything in sight.

Her eyes glowed with enjoyment of the comfortable furniture and intimate lighting that beckoned her nearer. But when she focused on the piano, a gleaming baby grand that anchored the room, he saw longing.

She approached it reverently, and let her fingers delicately trace its lines. 'You play.'

It was a statement of fact, and Daniel measured the emotion behind it.

'Yes,' he conceded carefully, 'I play. And you?'

Her face clouded. 'I used to play.'

'Show me,' he urged, exposing the keys. 'Play for me.'

Markie instinctively stepped away and hid both hands behind her back. 'No, I can't. It was—a very long time ago. I've forgotten how.'

'You never forget how to play a piano,' he argued, uncertain why it seemed so important that she touch the keys that had defined his life for the last fifteen years.

'I've forgotten.' Her voice was flat now and invited no argument. 'I was just a child and had access to the piano for such a short time——' She broke off as she remembered the foster home where she had found the piano. It was the fourth one she had lived in, and she had stayed just a few short months. But even at the age of seven, she had heard the first, unpractised notes from the piano and fallen in love. She had been determined to learn to play the instrument, seeking, as always, to fill up corners of her life. Those few months, more than any other, she had had a desperate need for fulfilment. By the time they took her away, she had learned to read music, learned to play a few simple songs.

It was a lie to say that she had forgotten how to play, for she carried that knowledge deep inside her. But it was something so personal to her, so tied up with loss and need, that she simply couldn't share it with a stranger.

A stranger. . .Daniel was a stranger to her, yet at times she felt she knew him well. It was the oddest thing. . .

'Markie?'

His voice brought her back to the present. 'Would you play for me, Daniel?'

He studied her in silence for a moment, perhaps looking for signs that she was merely being polite. What he found, Markie knew, was a real desire to hear the beauty of his music. Finally, he smiled slightly and nodded his head, taking a seat on the bench.

She leaned carefully against the piano, her hands pressed flat against the wood to feel the thunderous vibrations of the notes as they sliced through the air and moved through her body. She closed her eyes and waited.

There was a curious, pounding silence as she stood there, anticipating the first note. A moment passed, and then another, until she opened her eyes in question.

Her gaze was captured instantly by Daniel's curiously intent regard. In his eyes she saw confusion and something she struggled and failed to name as the silence danced between them. Nevertheless, she couldn't turn away from the possibilities.

Then, as if she had somehow answered an unasked question, Daniel nodded, just once, and struck the first chord. Then the rhapsody began. Markie felt it within and she felt it without. It could have lasted minutes or hours, she never knew, because it somehow transported her to a place outside of time. It was beautiful and sad and wise. And through it all, she was vitally aware that the magic was coming from Daniel. She listened and was enveloped in his magic.

When the music at last stopped, when the last note died away, when the final echo of the final vibration faded, she opened her eyes.

She didn't tell Daniel that it had been beautiful, although it had been. She didn't say that he was an accomplished pianist, although he most obviously was. Instead, she gave him two words.

'Thank you.'

His expression was wary. 'You know who I am, don't you, Markie?'

She smiled slightly. 'You're Daniel Reed.'

'How long have you known?'

'I'm fond of your music.' It wasn't an answer and it was. Daniel understood.

'You knew in the meadow.'

'Yes.'

His eyes narrowed. 'But you didn't say anything then.'

She looked honestly puzzled. 'What should I have said?'

He rose to his feet, impatience and puzzlement in every line of his body. 'You wouldn't even come home with me until I told you my name. But if you knew all the time——'

'It wasn't *knowing* your name I needed, Daniel. It was having you *tell* me. Do you understand the difference?'

'I suppose I do,' he answered after a considering moment. 'But why did you wait so long to tell me?'

'You didn't bring it up. I didn't see any reason for me to do so.'

He turned to study her minutely, looking, she assumed, for some sign of groupie fever or incipient hero-worship. Thinking this, she couldn't prevent a smile. Whatever she felt for Daniel, it had nothing to do with the fact that he was famous. It had to do with the man beneath the self-protective façade.

She shook herself mentally. *If* she felt anything for Daniel, she amended, that was what it would have to do with. But she didn't. Couldn't. Because Daniel, she knew, would somehow threaten her search.

'You said you spend six months during the winter up here. Do you use that time to write your songs?'

'Yes.' His response was flat, but Markie, interested, pressed on.

'And the rest of the year?' she probed, then proceeded to answer her own question. 'I suppose you work on the production of your releases, right? Recording, design, things like that. I know you don't tour any longer.'

The last remark fell into a bitter silence. Daniel stiffened angrily, his face expressing fierce irritation. Markie wondered what she had done to arouse such anger.

'Aren't you going to ask?'

Markie blinked at the rough tone. 'Ask what?'

His mouth twisted cynically. 'Why I stopped touring. Why I live up here in isolation. Why I lost interest in fame. Any of the above. All of the above.'

She knew. She didn't need to ask the question because she knew the answer. Listening to his lyrics, she sometimes felt that she knew the man who wrote them. 'If you want to tell me.'

He turned on her. 'Well, I don't. I don't owe you any explanation.'

'No,' she agreed calmly, 'you don't.'

'So you can just quit—what did you say?' he broke off his tirade in sheer astonishment.

'I said you don't owe me any explanation.'

Daniel studied her in total confusion, reading the unswerving honesty in her eyes. She didn't expect anything of him, he realised slowly. Hadn't even expected him to come for her when the storm moved in. Didn't want his explanations. Didn't want his fame. Didn't want his reflected glory. Didn't want—him.

For the first time for a long time, Daniel thought, he was face to face with a woman who wanted nothing from him. Wasn't it ironic that, for the first time ever, he wanted to give? Markie, he thought, would understand why he had left that other life behind. Markie would understand what he had found in his mountains.

But Markie, he realised, had no intention of understanding. She was a temporary stranger in his life. When the snow was gone, so would she be gone.

He squared his shoulders. 'If you don't mind, I have some work I need to do.'

It was, without a doubt, an invitation for her to leave his music-room. She took no offence. 'Of course,' she agreed, stepping away from the piano. 'I have some work of my own.'

His eyes narrowed briefly and she saw the question there, but he didn't ask. He didn't say anything as she turned and descended the stairs. But his eyes followed her until she was lost from view, and they were the colour of a storm at dawn.

Markie stood in the kitchen and thought of repayment. Daniel had dismissed the need with an impatience that she didn't understand, but she was not so easily swayed. She owed him. And while it was extremely doubtful that she would ever have the opportunity to save his life or offer shelter, she would do what she could. Beginning with. . .

She nodded her head decisively and headed for the utility-room. She searched methodically and found what she sought, then quickly donned her coat, gloves, and boots. She left the house soundlessly, just as the first notes of music drifted down from the loft, and set to work.

'What in hell are you doing?'

Markie tossed the shovelful of snow away and turned to face Daniel. She was breathless and flushed from cold and exertion, and a fine tremble weakened her arms. But she had cleared almost the entire path that led to the building that housed the generator, and the sense of accomplishment was heady.

Heady, until she saw the thunder in Daniel's eyes.

Carefully she lowered the shovel, surreptitiously propping herself up with it.

'I said——'

'I'm shovelling snow,' Markie interrupted, hoping her calmness would temper his anger.

It did not. His eyes flashing, he demanded succinctly, 'Why?'

'It must have been hard going to check on the generator through all that snow,' she explained reasonably. 'And I imagine you'll have to go out more than once. There's no point in risking injury or——'

'It's part of your pay-back, isn't it?' His mouth was grim. 'Dammit, Markie! I would have shovelled the path myself.'

'Of course,' she agreed. 'But now you don't have to. I'm almost finished.' She gestured to the small distance left between the cleared path and the building.

'You are finished,' he corrected, snatching the shovel from her hands.

Unfortunately, Markie had been resting all her weight against it. As her support was snatched out from beneath her, she stumbled forward. With lightning reflexes, Daniel released the shovel and grabbed for her. But he was off balance, and totally unprepared for the weight of her fall.

Together they tumbled into the high drift that Markie had created as she shifted snow to the side of the path. The snow met them, cushioned them, engulfed them as they sank into its frigid embrace.

On the bottom, Daniel took the brunt of the minor avalanche that resulted as the sides of their makeshift bed caved in and showered them with snow. Down his boots, in his shirt, around his neck it seeped like icy fingers.

Through snow-dusted eyelashes he looked up at

Markie in silence. His eyes were more eloquent than any words he could muster. Markie's mouth was tight, but not with dismay, Daniel realised ironically. She was biting her lips to prevent laughter. Her eyes danced with it, her body shook with it.

But there was no sound between them, nothing to break their gazes, until a small chunk of snow gave in to the demands of gravity and landed with a sound of soft apology on Daniel's nose.

He watched with almost clinical detachment as Markie's control broke and her laughter spilled between them. It started first in her stomach. He could feel in the intimacy of their position. His fingers itched to trace its path as it moved upward to her lungs, her breasts. . . Their sweet, soft weight jostled against him innocently as the laughter built and reached her throat. Her mouth quirked into a smile of pure enjoyment, and the laughter emerged. Soft, he thought again, somewhat hazily. And honest, like her.

'Oh, Daniel,' she managed weakly, smiling into his eyes, 'I'm sorry. I shouldn't laugh.' Cold fingers reached out to brush the snow from his face.

He caught her wrist easily, felt the steady beat of her pulse beneath his fingers. She wasn't laughing at him, he realised, but at them both. And her eyes, her lips, every part of her invited him to share the joke.

He shook his head. 'You have to be the clumsiest wild flower in existence!'

Markie shifted away regretfully, curiously aware of how good it felt to rest against his strength. She hadn't known that the hardness of muscle and bone could be so yielding, so comfortable.

'I'm really sorry,' she apologised penitently, scrambling to her feet. 'Let me help you up.'

Daniel studied her outstretched hands ironically. He

had little doubt that she could do just that. Quietly it came to him that those sweet hands could do a lot for him. . .

Silently he offered his hands and felt hers close around them. On his feet, he met her eyes. 'What was this supposed to pay me back for, Markie?'

'I thought I'd start in order,' she admitted cheerfully, letting her hands rest in his possession. 'This was supposed to be for letting me camp in your meadow. But the way things are going,' her brow wrinkled, 'I'm goihng to have start paying you back for my pay-backs!'

'Please, Markie,' Daniel entreated. 'No more pay-backs. I don't know if I could survive them.'

She smiled at him sweetly, gave his hands a reassuring squeeze. . .and made no promises.

Two days passed. . .slowly. A ragged caution hovered between them. Daniel retreated to his loft in the morning, leaving Markie to her own devices. Unspoken between them was a no-trespassing rule which kept Markie out of the loft, but not out of trouble.

'What in hell are you doing?'

It was, unfortunately, a phrase that was fast becoming familiar to Markie, as was the disbelieving, diverted, confounded tone in which it was uttered.

She had not given up her attempts to repay Daniel for his assistance, despite his pleas to the contrary. She stuck to her original plan of repaying his kindnesses in order, although she did concede that she would have to skip over repayment for his rescue until she had devised something of equal magnitude. Privately, she worried that there would never be such an occurrence and her debt would remain outstanding. Even the thought of accepting such charity made her painfully uneasy.

So in the face of this irate demand, like all the others over the past two days, she simply smiled. 'I'm chopping wood.'

Daniel shook his head despairingly. 'Why?'

'This is for that first night's shelter.'

'I told you I didn't want to be repaid, Markie. Dammit, I've told you that at least a dozen times now!' he exploded.

'Now, Daniel,' she soothed, 'let's not exaggerate.'

He began a furious count on his fingers. 'There was the time I found you rearranging my bookshelves——'

'To repay you for lending me your shirt and robe,' Markie inserted meticulously. 'I'm sorry you don't appreciate the rainbow effect I achieved.'

'It's not one of the more accepted methods in library science,' he told her a little desperately. 'I *liked* my alphabetical arrangement.'

Markie wrinkled her nose. 'Stuffy.'

With a visible effort, Daniel redirected his attention and continued to list her trespasses. 'Next came the— special dinner you prepared.' One hand rubbed unconsciously over his stomach.

Markie peeped at him through her lashes. 'To make up for the stew you made the first night. Are you feeling better yet, Daniel?'

He shuddered in memory. 'I've never had beef cooked that way before.'

Her brow furrowed defensively. 'What way?'

'You mean you don't know either?' he burst out, appalled all over again.

'Of course I know!' she defended fiercely. 'It was. . .blackened. Er—Cajun style.'

'Burnt,' he muttered beneath his breath.

'OK. I shouldn't have let myself be distracted by the elk I saw through the window. I did apologise.'

'And your attempt at laundry?' he prodded unkindly.

'That wasn't my fault!' she protested virtuously. 'Someone sneaked in when I wasn't looking and took one sock in every pair you own.' She eyed him suspiciously.

'Well, it wasn't me!' he denied. 'Markie, I'm wearing one grey sock and one pink sock. Pink!' he repeated disgustedly. 'Hell, before you did the laundry, I didn't *own* anything pink. Now I've got pink socks, pink shirts, pink jockey——'

Markie smiled cheekily. 'You needed some colour in your wardrobe.'

Daniel looked into her shining face and felt something in him gentle. Markie had brought colour to more than his wardrobe. She'd brought a rainbow to his life. The house echoed with her questions, her laughter, the force of her personality, where before it had only echoed with silence. Despite the casualty to his stomach and his clothes and his books and his solitude, that was something he couldn't regret.

'Let me help you with the wood,' he offered gruffly, reaching for the axe.

Markie shook her head. 'I'll only have to find another way to pay you back.'

Daniel blanched at the prospect. 'Oh God! Why can't you believe that I don't want you to repay me?'

She met his eyes steadily. 'Why can't you believe that I have to do it whether you want it or not?'

'We have to talk about this,' he told her severely.

'This sounds serious,' she noted, tongue in cheek. 'I know talking to me gives you a headache.'

'What makes you think that?' he probed carefully.

Markie watched him rub his temple and said nothing.

'The point is——' he began with strained patience, only to be interrupted by her determined tone.

'The point is that you saved me from a blizzard. You've opened your home to me, when I know you'd much prefer to be alone. I *owe* you, Daniel. And I always pay my debts.' Her chin tilted defiantly, challenge in her eyes.

Daniel stared into her upturned face, eyes focusing helplessly on the curve of her stubborn mouth. And even though it was set with determination, her mouth still looked incredibly soft and inviting. Inviting. . .

With sheer determination, he pulled his gaze from her lips. 'Fine,' he rumbled irritably. 'I rarely argue with a woman wielding an axe.'

'Well, if I'd known that I'd have picked it up days ago.' The threat was gentle and utterly sincere.

'Why don't you pick up some of these logs instead?' Daniel asked, reaching for some himself. 'We're almost out in the house.'

Markie smiled triumphantly and began to help. 'Which is why I was chopping wood in the first place—oh!' With a cry of pain, she suddenly dropped everything she held.

Daniel dropped his load as well, and reached for her with undisguised urgency. 'What? What is it? What's wrong?'

Markie held up her hand mournfully, presenting her palm for his inspection. 'I got a splinter.'

'Dammit,' he cursed, exploring her skin with exquisite gentleness, 'why aren't you wearing work gloves?'

'Because yours were about sixteen sizes too big,' she complained quietly, suddenly, violently aware of the touch of his fingers. Uncomfortable, she tried to pull her hand away.

Daniel tightened his hold. 'It's not my fault that you have ridiculously tiny hands.' He caressed her palm unconsciously. 'Look at this, Markie! You've got blisters from the axe.'

'I'm all right,' she insisted, curling her fingers protectively.

'Come inside,' he ordered roughly. 'We need to get that splinter out and put some ointment on the blisters.'

Markie peeped at him ironically. 'Florence Nightingale, I presume?'

Daniel pushed her towards the house. 'Right now, I'm all you've got.'

Markie thought, quite unwillingly, that right now he was all she wanted. The implications of that shook the roots of her much-prized independence and she came to an abrupt and unexpected halt in the middle of the pathway, causing Daniel to crash into her from behind.

She waited in patient silence while he finished a litany of every swear-word he knew, then turned to face him boldly.

'Daniel, we can't go on this way.'

'If you're referring to the dangerous imitation of Laurel and Hardy we've been indulging in——'

'I'm not,' she dismissed carelessly, then smiled consideringly. 'Although——'

Daniel rushed into speech. 'To what *were* you referring?'

'This—temporary strangers arrangement,' she answered exasperatedly. 'I'm no good at it. I don't *want* to be good at it. Can't we just be friends?'

She watched in fascination as his eyes clouded. Then he sighed, so faintly that she felt it more than heard it.

'All right,' he agreed at length, giving her a faint smile, 'let's be friends.'

Her eyes sparkled and she threw her arms around him in impulsive happiness. 'Thanks! Now, how do we do that?'

He drew away carefully. 'Hell, I don't know. I suppose we should start with patching up your wounds.' He studied her with an odd expression. 'That's what friends are for, aren't they?'

Markie's eyes sparkled. 'I could have used you a long time ago.' She showed him a scar at the base of her thumb and launched into a long and highly unlikley account of how she had acquired it.

Daniel listened with half an ear as he herded her gently towards the house. Anything, he thought, to get her away from that axe.

On another level entirely, he wondered what other scars Markie bore and how cleanly they had healed. Wondered if she had had a friend to bind them.

CHAPTER FIVE

THE declaration of friendship changed things between Daniel and Markie, but she would have been hard pressed to describe exactly how. Perhaps it was simply that a bit of the distance separating them was bridged, a fraction of the caution dissolved.

Because Daniel's offer of friendship meant much to her, Markie took pains not to alienate him with blatant attempts at repayment. Although still determined to balance the scales, she evolved a more subtle strategy. She no longer made a point of settlement on a one-for-one basis. Instead, she helped where she could, because she could. And she gave Daniel the solitude he seemed to need for his work.

The days had settled into a pattern. They met in the kitchen each morning for breakfast, which they prepared together. Over the meal, they were quiet or talkative, depending on their mood.

Lunch was a hit-or-miss meal. They made no plans to eat together, although sometimes their forays into the kitchen coincided. Around six o'clock, both gave up on their individual pursuits and they came together to prepare the evening meal.

After Markie's one attempt at making dinner alone, Daniel seemed loath to leave her in the kitchen unattended. She should have been indignant, she told herself in amusement. But the truth was that she enjoyed his company and his conversation, even if he did sometimes probe too deeply with questions she didn't want to answer.

After dinner they talked or read or went back to work, but this was the time that Markie enjoyed most. Daniel's moratorium on her presence in the music-room was lifted in the evening, and whatever they chose to do, they did together in the loft.

Inevitably, Markie learned much about Daniel during their time together. Breakfast time was a particular eye-opener, when he came in grumpy and vulnerable, needing coffee and conversation to rouse himself into coherency.

On one such morning, she stood at the kitchen window, enraptured by the vivid crispness of colour and air as the toast burned to cinders beside her. Daniel shook his head in silent resignation and disposed of the charred remains.

The day had dawned bright and clear and bitterly cold, continuing the pattern of snowy perfection.

'It's beautiful,' Markie whispered aloud.

'It's burnt beyond recognition,' he corrected, staring mournfully at the bread.

That brought Markie's attention back to him. 'It's——? Oh, Daniel, I'm sorry,' she apologised guiltily, spying the smoking mess in the sink. 'I was supposed to be watching the toast, wasn't I?'

He shrugged dismissively. 'You seemed more captivated by the morning.'

Her eyes lit eagerly. 'It's so clear outside. Maybe it's the snow that makes the sky look so blue. Every colour, every shape is so sharply defined——' She broke off at the expression on his face. 'I guess you're used to this.'

He shook his head. 'No, I never get used to it. But you talk as if you've never seen snow before.'

'I didn't see snow until I was eighteen years old,' she answered absently.

He watched her closely. 'Eighteen? Where did you grow up, Markie?'

A silence hovered between them, so infinitesimal that Daniel wondered if he hadn't imagined it.

'South Texas.'

He smiled. 'I thought I detected a bit of a drawl. Does your family still live there?' He knew he was pushing, felt her drawing away mentally if not physically, but it was important that he get solid information about Markie's past. It was a need he had been struggling with since that first day in the meadow, he recognised. A need Markie didn't seem eager to satisfy.

She evaded his question with a great lack of subtlety. 'I'll start some more toast.'

He watched her slip away. 'Markie——'

'It's OK, I promise I'll watch it this time.'

He sighed and dropped the subject. It had been the same yesterday, and every time they came together. Markie, he had discovered, would go to great lengths to avoid talking about her own past. At dinner the night before she had exhibited unexpected skill in filling every moment with talk of unrelenting trivialities, simply because he had had the audacity to ask whether she had any brothers or sisters.

Not that she had convinced him she was possessed of a trivial mind or uninteresting conversation. In Markie he sensed a depth and breadth of knowledge that could only have been enhanced by her travels. Yet that subject too she steadfastly refused to touch on.

'What about you, Daniel?' she asked over her shoulder, her voice bright. 'Where were you born?'

He gave in gracefully. 'Right here in Colorado—in Boulder. My parents were both studying for their doctorate degrees at the university.'

Markie winced. 'Doctorates?'

''Fraid so.' He smiled, thinking of his parents. 'They're teaching at a small private college in Maine now.'

'What do they teach?'

'Dad's a chemist, Mom's a physicist.' His voice was shaded with pride.

'You're close to them.' It wasn't a question. Markie could hear the love and respect in his voice, see it in his face. She struggled with quiet envy.

'Very close,' he confirmed, his eyes alight with curiosity.

Perhaps she hadn't hidden her reaction well enough to escape his attention. Because she wanted to distract him, and because she really wanted to know, Markie rushed another question. 'Was it hard for two scientists to understand that their son wanted to become a musician?'

'They never tried to pressure me into pursuing another career. But you know parents,' he said wryly. 'They worried that I wouldn't earn enough to maintain a decent lifestyle.'

Markie laughed involuntarily. Daniel's house was beautiful and spacious, but she knew that he could have built a palace and never counted the cost. He lived exactly as he wanted, comfortably and unassumingly. And she knew quite well that he had several million dollars at his disposal should he wish to indulge in any whim. It was really a shame, she thought regretfully, that she wasn't a gold-digging type of woman. But then she had enough money to indulge a few whims of her own.

'What do they think now?' she wondered.

'They're my biggest fans. They stood behind me when I spent eight months out of the year on tour, moving from city to city. And later——' He broke off. 'I don't see them as much as I'd like. We try to keep our relationship private so they won't be exposed to the kind of media coverage I've had to live with. But I know that they're always there when I need them, and I hope that they know the reverse is true.'

'You're very lucky.'

'Yes, I know.' He studied her thoughtfully. 'I wish you could meet them. They'd like you.'

'Well, sure,' Markie dismissed lightly. 'I was thinking of wandering over to the east coast this autumn. Maybe I'll look them up.'

Daniel's eyes narrowed. For some reason her casual response irritated the hell out of him. He wondered why.

But when Daniel was working, when there were no meals to prepare, no stove to stoke, no generator to check, Markie was left with empty hours to fill. So she went to work, as well.

On the fourth day of her stay, she sat at the kitchen table, her eyes focused blankly on a wall. She didn't actually see the wall, just as she no longer heard the music from the loft. Her mind was occupied with other matters. In front of her was a blank notebook. In her hand was a stubby pencil whose eraser she rubbed unconsciously against her bottom lip.

Daniel slipped into the chair across from her, his face alight with curiosity. An hour ago, when he had stopped for coffee, she had been in exactly the same position. Then, as now, she seemed totally unaware of his presence. He, however, was totally aware of hers, and that awareness had finally driven him from the music-room and back to her side.

'Markie.'

He waited, but she didn't even blink. He tried again.

'Markie, what are you doing?'

'Plotting a murder,' she answered absently, without so much as looking at him.

Daniel's brow kicked up as he considered this response. At length, he responded, 'I see. Was it something I said?'

She chewed the eraser briefly, eyes narrowing as she considered some intricate point.

'Something I did?'

She bumped back to reality at the dry question. 'Something you did? What are you talking about, Daniel?'

He leaned back, satisfied now that he had her full attention. 'Your murder plot, of course. Was it something I did?'

She blinked at him. 'Don't be silly! I'm not plotting your murder.'

He issued an exaggerated sigh of relief. 'So whose murder are you plotting?'

Markie cocked her head, as if she were listening for something. 'Aren't you playing the piano?' she asked at last.

Daniel thought the answer to that was rather obvious, but obliged none the less. 'No, I'm not. I was, but then I stopped.'

She nodded and began to make rapid notes on the paper in front of her. Daniel, with great forbearance, tried once again.

'What are you writing?'

She looked up briefly. 'I'm making notes for my book.'

'Book? You're writing a book?'

She shrugged. 'Sure.'

'You didn't tell me you were a writer,' he accused.

'Didn't I?' Markie questioned innocently, fooling neither of them. Each knew that she had little intention of sharing herself with him, although she understood the reasons far better than Daniel. 'I thought I had.'

'You're writing a mystery?' he pressed, inching closer in hopes of catching a glimpse of her notes.

'Umm,' she agreed, casually sliding her hand over the page in front of her to block his view.

'Are you going to try and sell it?' he probed interestedly.

She smiled at him with real amusement, thinking of her last three novels, each of which had graced the best-seller lists. 'I thought I might.'

'Maybe I could help,' Daniel offered. 'I read a lot of mysteries. Perhaps I could give you some advice.'

'That's very nice of you,' she replied doubtfully, somewhat taken aback by his avid interest. She had made a point of separating her professional life from her personal life, totally unwilling to give herself over to the public domain. She used a pseudonym and no one but her publisher could ever connect her with her books. So Daniel's offer, which was intended to be helpful, loomed as a threat in her eyes. 'But——'

'But——?'

'I'd feel strange about letting anyone see my book before it was finished,' she improvised hurriedly.

'Think of me as an editor,' he advised, sliding surreptitiously closer to her notebook.

'Daniel.'

He lifted his gaze expectantly and read the discomfort on her face. A platinum wall came up behind his eyes and he backed away immediately. 'I'm sorry.'

He was gone from the room before she could form a single word. Alone, she stared sightlessly at her notebook and scowled. He had pushed at the walls of her privacy and she had withdrawn behind them. It was a scenario that had repeated itself in one form or another through-out her life.

So why, now, did it feel so wrong? Why, now, did it feel so lonely behind those walls?

She had withdrawn from habit, Markie realised slowly. Because it was what she had done for as long as she could remember. She had automatically classified the offer as a threat. But Daniel was her friend, or was trying to be. Funny, she had asked for his friendship, but now discovered herself to be too inept to take it. And worse, far worse, too selfish to give her own.

Now, tentatively, she reached into herself and tried to understand what she felt. Frightened, she realised slowly, in a way that had nothing to do with the fear she had known for the last six years. She didn't think Daniel would change because of what she was, what she did. She didn't think that he would consider her to be less, or more, than he did now. A little sadly she realised that she didn't know what Daniel considered her to be.

With difficulty she asked herself if her real fear lay, not in Daniel's reaction to this deeper knowledge of her, but in her own. Once she shared this piece of herself, would she be hurt by the emptiness left behind? Would she be tempted to share more?

Whatever the outcome, Markie determined, she was going to offer this part of herself to Daniel. Not because of the hurt she had glimpsed in his eyes before he threw up a wall, although she felt that hurt inside herself even now. Not because she owed him for saving her life and providing a kind of warmth and shelter she had never experienced. No, she would give him this not out of guilt or obligation, but out of need. A need she didn't understand, but couldn't fight against. His. . .and hers.

With quiet determination she gathered her notebook and rose from the table. He would be in the music-room, she knew. She didn't know how she knew, exactly, for there was no sound to guide her. A part of herself that she simply couldn't acknowledge felt him there.

Briefly, she stopped in the living-room, collected what she sought, and climbed the stairs.

He was standing at the glass wall that overlooked the balcony and the frozen range beyond. He didn't turn when she crossed to his side, but she knew that he was aware of her presence. She stood beside him for a minute, marshalling her thoughts before she began.

'Daniel, there's something I want to show you.'

He shifted to smile at her faintly. She saw then that there was no anger in his eyes, no resentment in his response. Only—resignation. 'It's OK, Markie. I shouldn't have pushed like that. God knows, there are parts of me I've kept off limits to strangers: my land, my songs, my wild flowers.'

'I told you that I've never thought of you as a stranger.'

'We made a deal,' he reminded her. 'And temporary strangers should know better than to ask for things that they wouldn't give.'

Markie squared her shoulders. 'That deal is null and void, remember? We're friends now.'

'Yes,' he agreed almost soundlessly. 'Temporary friends.'

Quite desperately, she wanted to explore that comment, but drew herself away. Instead she told him, 'I realise that I haven't demonstrated the openness required by friendship, but that's going to change, starting now. You wanted to read what I've written. Here it is.' She handed him the notebook and watched as he took it helplessly. 'Of course, it's only a very rough outline and you can't decipher much of it. Perhaps these would tell you more.' She gave him three paperback novels—her novels that had made it to the best-seller lists. 'I found them on your bookshelf.'

Daniel looked at the books and drew a careful breath. He had read and enjoyed each book, and waited eagerly for the next to appear. Mark E. Smith was one of his favourite writers, a relative newcomer to the publishing world whose life was as mysterious as his works. But Mark E. Smith, he knew now, was not a man. Not a big-city, world-weary police detective as some speculated. Not a retired private investigator possessed of a way with words. Not a hard-boiled reporter, a senile Englishman, or an accountant from Duluth. Mark E. Smith was a wild flower on the wind, a stubborn, independent, delicate woman, an unwilling house guest, a temporary stranger. Mark E. Smith was Markie Smith.

Markie watched his face carefully and was frustrated by the cloaked response. She wanted to know what he thought, what he felt. She had given him this knowledge and he was giving her nothing. Suddenly, soberly, she remembered what he had said about asking for more than one was willing to give. She had denied that she was asking for anything, even to herself—most especially to herself. But she had lied. Did Daniel know that?

'I've read all five of your books,' he told her finally.

'The first two weren't as successful,' she said evenly, searching his eyes.

Daniel nodded. 'But no less intriguing. I imagine it's hard field to break into.' He paused, but Markie only nodded, so he continued. 'You're very good.'

She saw it. She finally saw the reaction in him, and took her first easy breath. There was no awe, no derision, no curiosity, no prying. She saw only honest appreciation for her writing skills, and it was all she wanted.

She smiled. 'I guess it's safe now for me to tell you that I have every one of your releases.'

Daniel blinked, surprised. She had never given any indication that she was a devoted fan. She had, in fact, said very little about his work. Now, finally, he understood, and that knowledge was like a very small flame leaping to life inside him.

'You didn't want to tell me about your writing for the same reason I didn't want to tell you about my music,' he murmured slowly. 'Because it's——'

'Private.' They said the word as one.

Daniel shook his head. 'It's an odd thing, isn't it? We share it with the whole world, with anyone who has the price of an album or a paperback, and yet. . .'

'Maybe we share the—the product,' Markie corrected. 'But we don't share ourselves.' She tilted her head quizzically. 'Not any more.'

'You never did,' he reminded her. 'There was never a picture of the author, never a biography.'

'And you don't any longer, ' she returned. 'Not since six years ago.'

'Why did you do this?' he demanded suddenly, waving the books at her. 'You've kept your secret for a long time, why tell me now?'

Markie's eyes were troubled. 'I don't know. I—needed to.'

He wanted to ask more. He wanted, suddenly, to ask everything. But he didn't. 'I'm glad you did,' he told her. 'You must have been very young when you wrote the first book.'

'I was eighteen.'

'Young,' he repeated.

'And not so young.'

Because he heard the emotion behind the flat rejoinder, he deliberately lightened the atmosphere. 'The offer's still open, you know. I'd be glad to proof your work.'

'That's very nice of you,' said Markie, playing along.

'Nice, hell!' Daniel scoffed. 'This is my big chance to get a preview on the next book by Mark E. Smith.'

Markie laughed. 'Well, actually, I could use some technical advice.'

His face brightened. 'Sure. We'll talk royalties later.'

She shot him a glance filled with indignant laughter and continued, 'My new book is going to be set at a mountain lodge in the Rockies. . .'

'And there's a snowstorm?' Daniel guessed, falling into the plot.

'And the guests are trapped, someone has disabled the snowplough, and people are disappearing, one by one. . .'

In the quiet room, with her enraptured audience, and the snow blanketing the outside world, Markie spun her web.

The next afternoon, Markie tossed her pen aside and stretched mightily. She had been writing since seven a.m. with nothing more than the occasional cup of tea to provide distraction. Now, seven hours and twenty-five pages later, her body was screaming for exercise. A walk in the snow, she decided, would be just the thing to revive her. Some solid food wouldn't hurt either.

She rose from the dining-room table where she had been working and cocked her head, listening. The drifting melody of Daniel's piano had ceased, but she had been so involved in her writing that she hadn't noticed until just now. Vaguely, she thought he had missed his lunch, as well. Moving into the kitchen, she decided to make an extra sandwich for him.

The cabinets easily yielded peanut butter and jelly, a staple of Markie's diet. She made several sandwiches for Daniel and cut them into neat triangles. She wouldn't think of interrupting him in his music-room, but she would leave the sandwiches on the table where they would catch his eye when hunger drove him into the kitchen.

She had just taken the first bite of her sandwich when Daniel strolled in. Unfortunately for Markie, she had made rather free with his supply of raspberry preserves and the first bite left a smear of sweet red fruit at the corner of her mouth.

Daniel watched as she desperately tried to swallow the thick peanut butter and smiled wryly. Her hands were smeared with jam as well, leaving her no way to deal with the stickiness on her lips.

With the best of intentions, he crossed to the table and bent over her. Their gazes held, hers bright with chagrined laughter and his indulgent. Casually, without thought, Daniel's finger dropped to her lips, picking up the sweet jam.

In the days that they had shared together, he had become accustomed to the effect of her touch. At least, that was what he told himself as he maintained a physical distance between them. He had even developed an explanation for the impact she had on his senses, something about loneliness and chemistry and propinquity. Unfortunately for his peace of mind, he only believed this explanation when he was maintaining his distance.

Carefully he withdrew his finger from her lips. The last fifteen seconds had just given the lie to hours of rationalisation. Her lips, her skin, her eyes proved him a liar.

'Peanut butter and jelly,' he managed wryly, taking a careful step away. 'You're such a child sometimes. Big eyes, sticky mouth!'

Markie wanted to open her sticky mouth to deliver an

indignant retort, but she hadn't quite managed to swallow the peanut butter yet. If she remembered correctly, it was the woman in her second foster home who had explained the importance of such social conventions.

Daniel read the fire in her eyes and simply smiled. 'I was going to make soup.'

Markie swallowed with great determination and gestured to the plate she had set out for him.

'I made you a couple of sandwiches.'

He grimaced good-naturedly and gestured to the mug in front of her. 'Are you drinking coffee?'

'Tea,' she corrected, indicating the pot on the table.

'OK,' he said easily, pulling a mug from the cabinet before taking a seat at the table. Absently, he brought his finger to his mouth, licking off the sticky jam he had lifted from Markie's lips. 'Raspberry.'

Her eyes met his, wary. A stark intimacy stirred between them as she watched his tongue lift the sweet taste of jam. Unconsciously, she licked her own lips, started at the taste of Daniel there. He must have the flavour of her on his finger, she thought with helpless fascination. She could almost feel that flickering tongue in a much more direct contact. Daniel and raspberry jam were a heady combination.

Daniel felt it too. A rough breath shook his chest before he dragged his eyes back to his mug.

'Are you finished writing for the day?' He threw the question out in a desperate attempt to shatter his own wayward thoughts.

Markie dropped her eyes. 'Yes. I thought I'd take a walk.'

His face expressed doubt. 'I don't know if that's such a good idea, Markie. With so much snow out there, it would be easy to fall. And you're not familiar with the terrain.'

Now more than ever, she needed to get out of the house. She felt the walls closing in on her, crowding her, pressing her closer to something she was reluctant to explore. 'I'll be careful,' she insisted quietly. 'I really need some. . .space.'

Daniel suppressed a sigh. Space. Hell, yes, he supposed she did. Five days of constant contact with another human being was probably five days more than she could stand. She was such a loner, and circumstances had forced her, forced them both, into a kind of intimacy best avoided.

But he couldn't just turn her loose outside, he thought frustratedly. The blankets of snow could hide treachery, especially from someone unaccustomed to the surroundings.

'I'll go with you,' he growled reluctantly, not meeting her eyes.

'That's not necessary,' Markie told him steadily. 'I can——' She broke off abruptly, remembering Daniel's unreasonable reaction to the particular phrase she was about to throw out. But, dammit, she *could* take care of herself, and it was best that they both remembered it.

Daniel felt her resistance and tried another tack. 'I could really use a break myself.'

Markie remembered the silent piano and her sympathy was instantly aroused. Better than most, she understood the frustration of being blocked creatively. It was something she, as a writer, had suffered from more than once, and she imagined that Daniel was no stranger to the problem either.

'All right,' she gave in abruptly. 'I'd—like your company.'

Daniel grinned at his sandwich and said nothing. Softhearted little thing, he thought tenderly. He had seen the sympathy on her face when he had dangled the bait in front of her. If only she knew that his frustration with his songwriting lay not in the inability to produce, but in the avalanche of overwhelming, unfamiliar emotions that were weaving themselves into his songs. Markie, he thought soberly, was responsible for that as well.

They finished their makeshift meal and swiftly cleared the dishes. In the utility-room they bundled themselves into their outer clothes. Although the snow had stopped, it was still bitterly cold outside and there was no hint of melting.

'I'm ready,' Markie announced happily, peering out at Daniel through layers of protective clothing.

'You look warm,' he commented in a choked tone, trying not to laugh aloud.

She grimaced cheerfully. 'I look like a red Michelin man!'

This time he did laugh and step nearer to brush the tip of her nose with his knuckle. 'You're much prettier.'

Markie was charmed. But before she could respond, he blinked and stepped away. With a sweeping gesture, he opened the outside door and motioned her out. 'Let's get this show on the road.'

She stepped out eagerly.

The day was glorious. A bright, cloudless blue sky contrasted sharply with the icy white world below. The air was crisp enough to cut through layers of warm clothing and instantly numb any exposed skin. Silent and somehow pure and new, it seemed like a world just born.

For Daniel, it was made more glorious by the uninhibited pleasure on Markie's face. He watched as she gambolled through the snow, like a playful fawn delighted by its untouched perfection.

'Daniel, it's beautiful!'

He met her bright, shining eyes and experienced a

fierce ache that caught him off guard. Beautiful. God, yes, so beautiful. For now the shadows were gone from her, and she was as joyful and uncomplicated as the summer sun.

Drawn by an unseen hand, he moved to her side. 'Come on,' he murmured with sudden decisiveness. 'I have something to show you.'

Even through the gloves they both wore, Markie felt the shock of his fingers curling around her own. And suddenly the day wasn't cold any more. There were no walls closing in on her, no needs crowding her. It was a feeling she had never before experienced, something she was too inexperienced to identify as the most special kind of freedom.

Willingly, she walked beside him. Every now and then she took an impulsive skip and watched the snow fly from their ploughing legs.

'You look like a lamb in spring,' Daniel confided, smiling at her antics.

'Nope,' she corrected. 'I'm a woman in spring. Right season, wrong species.'

He tightened his hand and they walked in silence for a while. Markie's mouth was curved in the most enchanting smile, bemused, happy, and her eyes were dreamy.

She would look like that after making love, he thought with a fragile ache. Soft and happy and satisfied. He would make sure she was satisfied.

Dear lord, what was he thinking? Markie would never be in his bed. There would be no lovemaking between them. She was still so wary, despite their new-found friendship. He would never breach the walls she hid behind. Doing so, he thought with unerring perception, would mean tearing down his own. They were temporary friends, and there could be nothing more. Soon Markie would be gone, a wild flower on the wind, letting go of spring. And Daniel would once again have his precious solitude.

'What are you thinking?' he demanded roughly, pushing that unsettling thought away.

Markie smiled at him companionably and squeezed his hand. 'I wasn't. I was just listening.'

He cocked his head. There was only silence.

'Don't you hear it, Daniel?' she questioned, her voice shaded with awe. 'The wind in the pines. Snow falling softly from the trees. Our footsteps smoothing the snow beneath us. A bird's wings beating against the air.'

'You're right,' he agreed gently. 'It's a regular Grand Central Station out here.'

Markie's mouth tilted with smiling reproof. 'Now, there's no need to make fun——'

Whatever she was going to say was lost as she tripped over a hidden rock and landed face first, full length, flat out in the snow. Daniel tried to save her, but the swiftness of the débâcle made it impossible. She released his hand in an instinctive bid to cushion her own landing.

It took him only a second to regain his own balance and he dropped on his knees at her side, concerned as he heard the muffled sounds from her throat. She was crying, he thought, panicked. She must be hurt, because Markie never cried. As gently as he could, he turned her over in the snow.

'Markie,' he began soothingly, brushing the snow away from her face. 'Sweetheart, are you OK?'

His answer wasn't the broken sob he expected. Instead, Markie's eyes snapped open, bright with laughter. She met his eyes and laughed in pure, uninhibited enjoyment.

Daniel watched her. He had never met anyone with the facility for laughing at themselves that she exhibited. She might be embarrassed, and her pride might be hurt, but she always found humour in herself when others would have fallen back on anger. Once he was sure that she was physically unharmed by her latest escapade, Daniel reached for humour as well.

'Making snow angels again?' he hazarded drily, his own eyes bright.

'What a great idea!' Wildly enthusiastic, Markie flattened herself in the snow and began scissoring her arms and legs with total abandon.

Daniel studied her cold-flushed face and wondered how a woman with such shadows could exude such light. And her light was everywhere, enveloping him, warming him, penetrating him.

'If you keep that up,' he warned, 'you're going to end up in China.'

She grinned and held out her hands demandingly. 'Help me up.'

He grabbed her hands and began to pull.

'Now be careful,' she chided. 'This is the most important part of snow-angel making, as I'm sure you know. We can't have any footprints showing through.'

'No, I didn't know,' he told her distractedly, their faces only inches apart. 'I've never made a snow angel before.'

'Never?' she was shocked. 'Daniel, why?'

'Sissy stuff,' he dismissed huskily, inching closer to her. 'Little boys build forts and have snowball fights.'

'Sexist,' she whispered, caught in the spell of intimacy. 'I bet I could throw a snowball with the best of them. And I'm not a little boy.'

'Hell, no,' Daniel agreed, his jaw tightening before he pulled away. 'Come on, Markie. You show me how to make a snow angel, and I'll show you how to build a fort. Deal?'

She eyed him curiously, wondering at his sudden

withdrawal. Wondering, as well, at the chill it left behind. 'Deal.' Taking a bracing breath, she pointed to a virgin patch of snow close to her own snow angel. 'Fall.'

He lifted a brow. 'Not, I assume, face down in your own inimitable style?'

Markie studied her gloves. 'Oh, sure. If you want to do it the boring way.'

'I do,' he assured her, before spreading his arms at his sides and falling backwards into the snow. 'Now what?'

With casual stealth, Markie moved to stand just over his left shoulder, out of view. 'Move your arms and legs like I did,' she directed. 'That will make the robe.'

'Robe?' he muttered beneath his breath. 'I'm not making any sissy angel!' None the less, he followed her command, flapping his arms and legs with secret enthusiasm. 'How's this?'

Markie didn't answer.

'Markie,' he demanded suspiciously, 'what are you doing?'

She started and carefully hid the small pile of snowballs she had been forming behind her back. 'Doing? I'm—er—drawing your halo.'

Daniel's eyes narrowed suspiciously, but he didn't challenge her.

'You'd better stop now,' she warned mockingly, 'or you're going to end up in China.'

He held out his arms imperiously. 'Help me up.'

'Help you up?' she panicked, looking at her small pile of snowballs.

'Well, we can't have any footprints on this dainty robe I made,' he pointed out helpfully.

She grimaced. This wasn't working out at all the way she had planned. She couldn't leave her weapons just sitting there, because Daniel would see them and that would surely ruin her surprise attack. And he deserved it, she assured herself roundly, thinking of the way he made fun of her for being so clumsy.

'Markie?'

'All right, I'm coming,' she answered his demand, quickly making her decision. As silently as she could, she began to stuff snowballs into the pockets of her jacket. But they were small pockets or else, she thought vexedly, she had made extraordinarily large snowballs. Philosophically, she slipped the remainder of her munitions inside her jacket and prayed that Daniel wouldn't comment on the lumps. Satisfied at last, she zipped her jacket carefully and moved to stand at his feet.

'OK, on the count of three,' she directed, offering her hands. 'One. . .two. . .'

'Three!' Daniel completed, surging to his feet with such deliberate force that she was sent tumbling backwards in the snow. With great relish, he landed spread-eagled on top of her and felt the snowballs flatten beneath her jacket.

'Oh!' yelped Markie, helpless to prevent the frozen mounds of snow from seeping through her clothes to her skin. 'You did that on purpose!'

Daniel propped his head in one hand and looked down at her with twinkling eyes. 'Did what?'

'You crushed my snowballs——!' she began hotly, only to break off as she realised that she was admitting to treachery.

He assumed an unbelievably innocent expression. 'Did you have snowballs in your jacket, Markie?'

'You know I did,' she grumbled, reaching towards her pockets under the guise of pulling her jacket free of her body.

'I heard the zipper,' he admitted contentedly, waggling a free finger under her nose. 'It's not nice to plan sneak attacks on——'

Markie's fingers closed over a miraculously unbroken snowball in each pocket. With a battle cry of vengeance, she brought both hands out and crushed her icy weapons against the sides of his face.

His lecture halted immediately and a martial gleam flashed in his silver eyes. Markie saw it and rushed into panicked speech, interspersed with uncontrollable giggles.

'Now, Daniel, you deserved that for what you did to me. I've got snow down my shirt—— No! Oh, Daniel, no!'

Daniel didn't even bother with forming snowballs. He simply scraped up great handfuls of snow and began shovelling it over her prone body.

The fight turned into a free-for-all of epic proportions. They rolled in the snow like children, first one, then the other in a dominant position.

Exhausted, energised, invigorated, Markie manoeuvred herself over Daniel and threatened him with a massive handful of frigid white powder.

Through snow-dusted lashes, he peered up at her, a foolish smile on his mouth. 'Do you give up?' he demanded, puffing.

'I'm in control here,' she pointed out with a great deal of gentleness.

With a single, twisting movement, Daniel flipped her on to her back and straddled her hips. 'You were saying?'

Markie blinked. Odd, how right it felt to be cushioned against the snow and against Daniel, to play with him with such innocence and abandon. There had not been enough of that in her life. Had not, she corrected honestly, been any of that in her life since Griff.

Daniel saw the flicker of pain and eased his hold. 'Markie?'

She met his eyes and felt something warm and soft

NO RISK, NO OBLIGATION TO BUY...NOW OR EVER!

GUARANTEED

PLAY "ROLL A DOUBLE" AND GET AS MANY AS SIX GIFTS!

HERE'S HOW TO PLAY:

1. Peel off label from front cover. Place it in space provided at right. With a coin, carefully scratch off the silver dice. This makes you eligible to receive one or more free books, and possibly other gifts, depending on what is revealed beneath the scratch-off area.

2. You'll receive brand-new Harlequin Presents® novels. When you return this card, we'll rush you the books and gifts you qualify for ABSOLUTELY FREE!

3. Then, if we don't hear from you, every month we'll send you 6 additional novels to read and enjoy. You can return them and owe nothing, but if you decide to keep them, you'll pay only $2.24 per book—a savings of 51¢ each off the cover price.

4. When you subscribe to the Harlequin Reader Service®, you'll also get our newsletter, as well as additional free gifts from time to time.

5. You must be completely satisfied. You may cancel at any time simply by sending us a note or a shipping statement marked "cancel" or by returning any shipment to us at our expense.

You'll look like a million dollars when you wear this elegant necklace! It's a generous 20 inches long and each link is double-soldered for strength and durability.

"ROLL A DOUBLE!"

PLACE LABEL HERE

SCRATCH HERE

SEE CLAIM CHART BELOW

106 CIH ACJ2

YES! I have placed my label from the front cover into the space provided above and scratched off the silver dice. Please rush me the free book(s) and gift(s) that I am entitled to. I understand that I am under no obligation to purchase any books, as explained on the opposite page.

NAME

ADDRESS   APT.

CITY   STATE   ZIP CODE

CLAIM CHART

	4 FREE BOOKS PLUS FREE 20" NECKLACE PLUS MYSTERY BONUS GIFT
	3 FREE BOOKS PLUS BONUS GIFT
	2 FREE BOOKS

CLAIM NO. 37-829

HARLEQUIN "NO RISK" GUARANTEE

- You're not required to buy a single book—ever!
- You must be completely satisfied or you may cancel at any time simply by sending us a note or a shipping statement marked "cancel" or by returning any shipment to us at our cost. Either way, you will receive no more books; you'll have no obligation to buy.
- The free book(s) and gift(s) you claimed on this "Roll A Double" offer remain yours to keep no matter what you decide.

If offer card is missing, please write to:
Harlequin Reader Service, 3010 Walden Ave., P.O. Box 1867, Buffalo, N.Y. 14269-1867

DETACH AND MAIL CARD TODAY!

BUSINESS REPLY MAIL
FIRST CLASS MAIL   PERMIT NO. 717   BUFFALO, NY

POSTAGE WILL BE PAID BY ADDRESSEE

HARLEQUIN READER SERVICE
3010 WALDEN AVE
PO BOX 1867
BUFFALO NY 14240-9952

NO POSTAGE
NECESSARY
IF MAILED
IN THE
UNITED STATES

and aching welling deep inside her. Frightened, she pulled away. 'You—were going to show me something,' she reminded him jerkily.

'Right.' Slowly he got to his feet, his gaze fixed on her. Without a word, he offered his hand.

Markie studied him with an unfamiliar need, searching for answers to questions she was afraid to voice. But the answers weren't in Daniel's eyes, and she was left with only her instincts to guide her.

She put her hand in his and felt his fingers tighten briefly.

'It's OK, sweetheart,' he promised softly. 'We'll work it out.'

Daniel took her to the wild flower meadow where he had first found her. The storm had left it smothered in snow, almost unrecognisable as the sweet spring field she had known. More than anything it brought home the knowledge of what would have happened to her had Daniel not come back.

'My tent was here,' she murmured, pointing to a waist-deep drift of snow.

Daniel tightened his fingers and pulled her away, towards a small huddle of pines standing guard over a frozen stream.

'That's not what I wanted to show you.' He knelt in the snow and drew her to his side. 'Look.'

Markie followed his pointing finger. Here in the shelter of the trees, the snow was not as thick on the ground. Through the patches of white and pine needles she saw a fragile splash of yellow. Amazed, she caught her breath and drew nearer.

'It's a flower,' she whispered, her eyes racing to Daniel. 'It survived that storm.'

He nodded, one long finger caressing a delicate petal.

'It's called a snowflower. It grows wild and thrives in the harshest places.'

'But it looks so fragile!'

'True beauty,' Daniel murmured quietly, reminding her of her comment about true beauty never being fragile.

Markie smiled in the soft, quiet way that made him ache. 'True beauty, Daniel.'

CHAPTER SIX

AFTER dinner that night, Daniel and Markie returned to the music-room. Daniel fiddled with the complex stereo components sheltered behind the wood cabinets on the east wall and soon the soothing strains of a Chopin prelude filtered from the speakers.

Markie curled up in front of the fireplace, lost in thought. She barely heard the music and was, for once, almost unaware of Daniel's presence.

Because she looked so distant when he needed her near, he asked, 'What are you thinking about?'

She answered, though her eyes remained fixed on the flames dancing in the grate, 'Time. . .coincidence. . . fate.'

'Oh.' His tone implied that he had known the answer all along. 'On a full stomach?'

This time she did look at him, sending a faint smile over her shoulder. 'I was thinking about how odd it is that we should meet.'

'Odd?' he queried.

'It seems as if our lives have been running on different paths since. . .'

'Six years ago,' he supplied soberly.

'Yes, six years ago.'

'March the twenty-seventh.' Daniel's voice was soft, distracted.

Markie stared at him blankly. 'How did you know that?'

He met her gaze curiously. 'Know what?'

'March the twenty-seventh. That's the day I left Texas. It was my eighteenth birthday.'

'Six years ago, on March twenty-seven, I performed at my last concert and came home,' he told her slowly. 'Not such different paths, after all.'

'That's incredible!' she managed faintly. 'I started travelling and you stopped.' She studied him closely, noting that the anger that had greeted her first mention of his aborted career was absent. Because she needed to know, she risked the question. 'Will you tell me why you stopped?'

He met her eyes sombrely. 'Will you tell me why you started?'

Her face shadowed. 'Pay-back, Daniel? I thought you weren't interested in that game?'

'I'm not,' he answered grimly. 'I just thought—oh, hell——!' He broke off harshly and reminded himself not to push. 'Six years ago I was—very successful.' It was an appalling understatement. Six years ago he had been riding the crest of a wave that had launched him into superstardom. A string of chart-topping singles and back-to-back platinum albums had turned him into one of the most popular musicians of the decade.

'I started touring when I was nineteen. Nineteen,' he repeated disgustedly. 'Hell, I was just a kid! I needed to sing my songs and know that I could touch people, needed the sense of belonging I got from that.'

Markie gave a little lop-sided smile. That much she understood, for it was what she received from her writing. The sense of acceptance was a strong lure, however subconsciously one sought it.

Daniel read her eyes and nodded in acknowledgement. 'You understand that, don't you, Markie? But for me, touring was a trade-off. It gave to me, but it took as well—so assiduously that I barely realised it at first. And then so completely that I was left feeling. . .incomplete.'

'Your privacy.'

He nodded, unsurprised by her perception. 'Yes, my privacy. You see, I couldn't separate myself from my music. I thought my songs needed me to give them voice, to make them real. They didn't, of course. But it took me a long time to understand that, and by that time the tables had turned. I needed the songs to make me real, to be my voice. I lost track of my priorities, lost track of myself, I guess.'

'I don't understand.' The man he described was not the man she was coming to know. Daniel was one of the steadiest people she had ever met. He knew what was important, knew himself, in a way few did. It was part of him she found most attractive.

He struggled for the words to explain. 'I travelled from city to city, until I couldn't remember where I was. I stayed in hotel rooms that all looked the same. I covered thousands of miles and performed for millions of people, until the spectacle of my performance became more important than the substance of my music.'

Markie's face was sombre with understanding. 'So you quit.'

'I was tired—God, so tired of giving over little pieces of myself to cities and hotel rooms and faces I couldn't remember.' Even thinking of those days hurt Daniel, but he pressed on. 'Yes, I quit touring. I needed time to rebuild what I'd given away so cheaply.'

'That's when you built this house.'

'Yes,' he concurred, 'that's when I built my home. In a way, I think this is what I was looking for all along, in all those cities, all those faces.'

'Home.' Markie's voice was almost soundless.

'Now I write my songs and let them stand alone.'

'But you record them,' she protested.

'Yes, I record them. But I do it because it brings me pleasure. I don't need the instant affirmation and sense of belonging I used to get from a crowd. I've got that here.' Lightly, he touched his temple.

Markie reached out to lay her hand directly over his heart, and felt its tempo against her skin. 'And here.'

Daniel took her hand. 'Haven't you heard, Markie? Home is where the heart is.'

She nodded jerkily, aware of the warmth of his hand against her own. 'I've got a theory, you know. About home.'

'Care to share it?'

She was suddenly trembling, because she had never given this much of herself to anyone before. Yet she knew that she was going to share it with Daniel. He, more than anyone, would understand.

'I think that everybody has a home,' she began earnestly, 'but that it's hardly ever the place they were born. It's too easy to settle for that, but I can't.' Her eyes caught fire. 'I *can't*. Out there somewhere is my home: a place where I belong, a place that needs me to make it complete.' And in turn, she thought, it will complete me.

Daniel understood instantly, even the things she didn't say. 'That's what the last six years have been about, isn't it, Markie? All this time you've been looking for a home.'

'That's why I envy you,' she admitted softly.

'Why?'

'Because you found your place,' she told him simply. 'You found your home.'

'No,' he corrected flatly, his eyes intent. 'Markie, I *built* my home. There's a big difference.'

'You don't understand,' she protested.

'I understand that six years is a long time to search for something.'

'However long it takes, it will be worth it.'

He measured her closely. 'What is it you left behind?'

Markie almost flinched, but stopped herself in time. She didn't question Daniel's skill in jabbing her weak point, but she wondered at his knowledge of its location. She must have given up more of herself over these past days than she had thought. Now she met his watchful gaze and knew that she could not give up any more.

'It's late, Daniel. I think I'll go to bed.'

She left him alone in the music-room, left his too-knowing eyes and questions. But long after she had turned off her bedside lamp, Daniel echoed in her mind.

When there was nothing to do, when Daniel couldn't play his music for thinking of Markie, when Markie couldn't write without thinking of Daniel, they came together. And because they couldn't give each other words without becoming vulnerable, a subtle game evolved between them. And they learned to play the game within other games.

The played chess. Every word was planned as intently as every move.

Daniel eyed the board. 'Do you like travelling, Markie?'

Her eyes skittered to his face, caution in their depths. 'It serves its purpose,' she answered at length.

'Does it?'

Her mouth tightened, but she didn't respond to the challenge.

Long minutes passed. The next gambit was Markie's.

'Daniel, do you think things happen for a reason?'

He watched her finger a bishop. 'I think that we have

something to learn from everything that happens,' he responded carefully.

'What about us?'

'Us?'

'Our situation,' she clarified. 'Do you think that we have something to learn from being together?'

Daniel smiled into her eyes. 'I've never doubted it for a second, Markie.'

Markie thought about that as her bishop took his knight. She had never doubted it either.

Minutes passed. Pieces were won and lost, strategies formed and abandoned.

Markie risked another move.

'When you were travelling,' she began quietly, 'did you ever get lonely?'

'Yes,' he answered flatly.

'But there were people around you.'

'Fans,' Daniel conceded. 'Roadies, agents, friends, musicians, groupies. I was rarely alone, never ignored. And I was so lonely sometimes that it hurt.'

She studied the board with unseeing eyes. 'Logically, I've always known that loneliness has nothing to do with being alone. But sometimes,' she admitted wistfully, 'over the years, I've caught myself thinking that if I just had someone to talk to, someone to——'

Daniel waited, but she didn't finish the statement. 'You've been lonely.'

She didn't answer.

'Are you lonely now?'

For a moment, it was as if she had forgotten to breathe. Utter and complete stillness settled on her. Then slowly, her head rose, her eyes searching for and holding his. Daniel saw something there: confusion, recognition, denial.

But Markie didn't answer.

For the moment, her silence was enough. And Daniel began to refine his strategy.

Markie propped her chin in her hands and sighed discontentedly. She was blocked. She hated it when this happened. Staring into the flames dancing in the fire-place, she reviewed her options. Nothing seemed quite. . .right.

Daniel stood at the entrance to the room. It wasn't the piano gleaming softly in the firelight that drew his eyes. It wasn't the breathtaking view of endless mountains past the windows that called to him. It was Markie, and it was a phenomenon that he was becoming accustomed to. Over the past week she had become a sharp edge buried in his mind. Innocently, unknowingly, she commanded his attention, reshuffled his priorities, cut into his protective walls.

He studied her as she lay curled up on the floor, her ever-present pen and notebook nearby. She had taken to working in his music-room, there in front of the fire-place. It never seemed to bother her when he joined her, sitting at his piano, picking out fragments of songs. At times, she barely seemed aware of his presence, but Daniel was always aware of her. He had developed to an art the skill of watching her without turning from the keyboard. Sometimes he thought he knew every breath she drew, every emotion that she felt.

Now, even across the room, he felt her frustration, heard it in her sigh, saw it in her body. Moving into the room, he determined to know more.

'How're you doing, Markie?'

She smiled at him half-heartedly as he dropped to the floor at her side. 'Not so good.'

Daniel made a point of peeping ostentatiously at her notebook. 'Working on the book?'

'Trying,' she corrected.

'Writer's block?' he diagnosed commiseratingly.

She shrugged. 'Not really. It's more a matter of. . .logistics.'

Daniel raised one eyebrow. 'I'm intrigued.'

This time Markie's grin was honest. 'I've always been intimidated by logical minds.'

'Understandable,' he responded drily. 'We're always wary of those things of which we have no pesonal knowledge.'

'Ooh, nasty!' she reproved. 'Just because I had trouble with one little recipe——'

'Markie, your cake exploded!' Daniel reminded her incredulously.

Markie dissolved into laughter, barely able to translate her thoughts into words. Finally, through uncontrolled giggles, she managed to gasp, 'It wasn't a cake, it was a *bombe*.'

Daniel shook his head, an unwilling smile tugging at his lips. 'Whatever it was, logic didn't enter into its creation.'

Her eyes rounded innocently. 'The recipe didn't call for logic. Not even a teaspoonful.'

'Good. You don't have a teaspoonful to spare.'

Markie sighed in agreement. 'True. Unkind, but true.'

'It makes me wonder how you write such fiendishly clever novels.'

'That's different,' she insisted. 'In my novels, I control everything: characters, motivations, thoughts. I poke and prod and twist and cheat until I'm satisfied. In reality,' she observed wryly, 'I've come to discover that ingredients don't so readily yield to manipulation. Flour and eggs are intractable and unimaginative things.'

Daniel couldn't resist threading one hand through the

length of her silky hair and giving a gentle tug. 'It's OK, wild flower. I like you just the way you are.'

Her eyes drifted to his, aware and curiously arrested as they searched his face. She saw it in the set of his mouth, the warmth of his eyes; a gentleness, an honesty that echoed his words.

Then he blinked, and every sign of emotion was blanked from his face in that instant. 'So what's got you stumped?'

Markie drew her eyes back to her notebook and grimaced. 'My murderer is about to strike, but I have to get two of the characters to vacate the room first.'

'So what's the problem?'

She shifted uneasily. 'They're—er—tied up.'

'Literally?'

'No!' Considering the content of the scene she was struggling with, that question caused a fiery red to mount in her cheeks. 'I meant that they were—involved in something.'

'OK,' he soothed, reacting to her defensive posture. 'What "something" are they involved in?'

Markie stared at her fingers with great intensity. 'They're—er—mknglv.'

'Mknglv?' Daniel repeated blankly. 'What's that? Quit muttering, Markie.'

Markie closed her eyes and enunciated clearly, 'They are making love. I'm having a problem with the logistics of it.'

He laughed at her with his eyes. 'It's all right, wild flower. I'll explain it to you. You see, in nature there are birds and bees——'

He broke off, choking with laughter, as she turned vengeful eyes on him. A hefty shove from her sent him toppling flat out on the carpet, and he simply lay there, staring at the ceiling and laughing himself silly. Not a long road, in Markie's estimation.

'That's *not* what I'm having trouble with,' she informed him imperiously, cutting through his mirth.

'Right.' Daniel gathered his breath. 'What's the problem?'

'I told you, logistics. They're sitting on the floor——'

'On the floor?'

She sent him a quelling glance. 'In front of the fire-pl——' She broke off abruptly as her eyes skittered towards the fireplace that she and Daniel bracketed.

'In front of the fireplace,' he parroted calmly. 'Then what?'

Markie closed her eyes and cursed silently. There was obviously no easy way out of this. Daniel was intent on helping her straighten out this plot point. Besides, she told herself righteously, she had no cause to be embarrassed! She was writing fiction, with no personal bearing at all. Surely he wouldn't think. . .surely she wouldn't. . .?

She opened her eyes and met his. Very calmly, without a hiccup, she outlined the problem. 'They're in front of the fireplace when they begin to kiss. Things move along rapidly. I have to find some way to get them from the carpet to the bedroom so the murderer can have the room.'

'*That's* what you're hung up on?'

Her expression was fierce. 'That's what I'm hung up on.'

'Can't you give these people a break?' Daniel asked with amusement. 'Let the murderer strike later. Leave them where they are.'

She blinked. 'The carpet would be uncomfortable.'

'This carpet isn't,' he pointed out reasonably.

'But you're just sitting on it,' she demurred. 'If you

were lying on it, with the weight of someone else over
you——'

'Let's see,' he suggested accommodatingly, grabbing
her hand.

Before she knew what was happening, before she had
a chance to protest or challenge, he was flat on his back
on the carpet and she was draped over him like a blanket.
From chest to toes, she was pressed against him, gravity
deepening the intimacy. She was shatteringly aware of
his hardness and his strength as her softer form seemed
to melt into him. Briefly, for one treacherous second,
she wondered what it would be like to let it happen, to
flow into him without a fight.

Then, because she was a strong woman and too aware
of the risk she courted, she stiffened. 'Daniel, what are
you doing?'

He studied her lovely face, just inches from his own,
and tightened his arms unconsciously. 'I'm not uncomfortable,' he told her, shifting a little as though easing a
sudden pain. 'That is, the carpet isn't uncomfortable,
even with your weight on me. It's—soft.' His fingers
brushed at her waist almost hypnotically. 'Very soft.'

She swallowed drily. 'Daniel, it's very good of you to
be concerned about my book——'

'I'm a hell of a guy,' he agreed solemnly.

'Be that as it may,' she pressed on determinedly, 'I
don't think I'll leave my hero and heroine on the floor.'
She pushed insistently against his hard chest.

Daniel sighed and opened his arms, watching calculat-
ingly as she retreated several feet and began straightening
her shirt. 'That still leaves you with the task of getting
them into the bedroom,' he pointed out.

She didn't even look at him. 'I'll think of something.'

'Could they walk?' he suggested, too delighted with
the effect the subject was having on her to let it go.

She sighed doubtfully. 'After they've been rolling around on the floor for thirty minutes? I think her knees might give out.'

'Thirty minutes!' he repeated. 'Forget about her knees. Your poor hero probably couldn't even *get* to his knees!'

Markie ignored him totally. 'Besides, it's not—romantic enough.'

'There's more to romance than being swept away by passion, you know. His voice was oddly solemn. 'I think it's damn romantic for two people to consciously make the choice to be together.' He focused on her thoughtfully. 'Of all people, Markie, I would have thought that you would understand that. Romance is partnership, not conquest.'

Her face was tense, her eyes searching and intent when she turned to him. 'Do you really believe that, Daniel?'

His answer was soft and steady. 'I really do, Markie.'

She studied him in silence for long moments, trying to sort through the feelings he engendered. In her head, she knew it would be better—safer—to walk away from him now, to maintain the distance between them. In her heart, she knew that distance was rapidly becoming a thing of the past.

With one final effort, she scooped her notebook up and rose to her feet. 'I'd better start dinner.'

He watched her take the first step away and knew he couldn't allow a second. They were far beyond the point now when he could pretend it didn't matter.

'Markie——'

She whirled to face him, and the silent fear in her eyes, the tension in her body, halted his challenge. Instead, he sighed and looked away. His gaze lit on a small photograph at his feet that must have fallen from her notebook as she stood.

He offered it to her. 'I think you dropped this.'

Curiously, she didn't reach for it immediately. She seemed to be torn with conflicting emotions. He saw the need to run, yet something held her back. Whatever it was, he knew it was something she had not shared with him.

He waited in silence, and finally she spoke. Her voice was small, the words reluctant. 'That's me. . .and Griff,' she nodded towards the picture in his outstretched hand.

Daniel studied the photograph for the first time. The girl was much too thin. Her long dark hair was pulled away from a face that was younger but no less proud than the one she presented today. Her chin was tilted at a defiant angle, but her eyes were shadowed, bewildered. Markie at the age of six. Beside her was a young man, perhaps ten years her senior. He too had a stubborn jaw, but his face was hard. Cynicism thinned his lips and aged his eyes. If there was any softness in that too-old face, it was in his regard for the little girl at his side. There was protectiveness in his stance beside her, caution in the distance he maintained.

'Your brother?' Daniel asked quietly, though he knew already that it was not.

'No,' Markie answered, finally taking the picture from his hand. 'Not my brother.'

'You don't have a family, do you, Markie?' Daniel didn't want to hurt her, didn't want to press, but it was time, past time, that he knew the answers. Perhaps those first words would be easier coming from his lips.

Markie must have sensed it as well. 'No, I don't. My mother gave me up when I was three years old. I grew up in foster homes.'

For Daniel, it explained much: the odd shadows that clouded her face when her childhood was mentioned, the quiet strength of purpose and self-knowledge so rare in one her age, and her seemingly overwhelming obsession for a home, a place to belong. 'You were never adopted?'

'My—mother never got around to signing those papers before she left.' Her smile lasted for perhaps a quarter of a second. 'Maybe she intended to come back for me some day.'

'Do you blame her for letting you go?'

Markie's brow furrowed. 'Blame her? No, I don't blame her. She had a decision to make and she made it. Who's to say that I'm not better off because of it?'

'Do you ever think of finding her?' Daniel was aware that he was treading in a potential minefield of unresolved emotion.

'No.' There was no anger or bitterness in the denial. 'She let go of me. I let go of her. Some things aren't meant to be.'

'What about your father?'

'My birth certificate listed his name as John Smith.' A shadow darkened her eyes. 'One step above "unknown". I guess she didn't know.'

'And Griff?' asked Daniel.

This time her smile was less fleeting. 'Griff. . . We shared a foster home for almost eight months. It was the longest either of us had ever been in one place. I like to think we were good for each other.'

'He didn't have a family?'

'Just. . .me,' she mused sadly. 'Just for those eight months. He was ten years older than me and I adored him. He let me trail around after him and always took the blame when I got in trouble. Just like a real brother.'

Daniel watched her finger gently trace the image of her friend. 'What happened after those eight months?'

She shrugged, carefully blanking all emotion from her face before looking up. 'The family we were living with moved out of state. We were sent to different homes.'

'But you kept in touch with Griff.' It wasn't a question.

'I wrote to him every week,' she confirmed, then issued a pained laugh. 'It must have been just fascinating for poor Griff to wade through my seven-year-old scrawls. He was almost a man by then.'

Daniel stared at the hard face in the photograph and thought that Griff had grown up long before then.

'I got letters back from him, intermittently, for almost a year,' Markie continued. 'And then they stopped.'

'Stopped?' He frowned. 'Why?'

'It was time,' she explained, vaguely confused by the question.

'Time?'

'Griff was released from the foster-care programme, released from state custody. He was out on his own. He didn't need any reminders of those years.' There was nothing but acceptance and lingering affection in her tone.

'Did he tell you that?' Daniel demanded incredulously, angered by the seemingly blatant cruelty of the man Markie had thought of as family.

'He didn't have to. I understood.'

'Damned good of you,' he rejoined sarcastically. 'Perhaps you could explain it to me.'

'Daniel, he gave me what he could, when he could. He helped me over a rough period. It was his time then.'

'Have you heard from him since?'

She shrugged. 'No. But I think he's OK. Griff is the kind of person who would have found his place.'

'Markie. . .' Daniel ached for her and she heard the emotion in his tone. Stiffening, she backed away.

'Don't you dare feel sorry for me, Daniel Reed! I don't need your pity.'

'I don't pity you,' he denied softly. 'But I hurt for that little girl with her bewildered eyes and stubborn chin.'

'Well, don't,' she told him shortly. 'She made out just fine, you know. She grew up to be very self-sufficient and independent. She doesn't——'

'Need anything from me,' Daniel finished for her, his mouth twisting at the familiar refrain.

She held his eyes earnestly. 'Daniel, don't feel sorry for me. Growing up in those foster homes——'

'How many foster homes?' he interrupted in a softly driven tone.

'That doesn't matter,' she insisted, frustrated.

'Doesn't it?' he pressed. 'Then tell me how many.'

She sighed and answered. 'Thirteen.'

Daniel's jaw hardened. 'Thirteen,' he repeated. 'Thirteen between the ages of three and eighteen. And where did you go in between times, Markie? Where did you stay then?'

This time she didn't answer.

'Forget it,' he dismissed. 'I can guess.' God, could he guess! 'You should be bitter, Markie, but you seem— thankful, instead.'

'I am thankful,' she insisted softly. 'How could I be bitter? I have so much, Daniel. Not in spite of my childhood, but *because* of it. When I find my place, I'll have everything. And I'll be happy.'

'When you find your place. . .' he repeated, searching her eyes. 'It's very important to you, isn't it, Markie?'

'Everyone has a place,' she told him resolutely. 'I need to find mine.'

'And that's what these last six years have been about?' he persisted doubtfully. 'Finding your place?'

She shifted, sensing his doubt. 'You sound disbelieving.'

'Confused,' he corrected. 'How can you find your place when you never stay still?'

'I'll know it when I see it,' she told him steadily. 'Until I find it, I'll keep looking.'

'Six years is a long time to look.'

'What are you saying?' she challenged.

'Maybe you're looking in the wrong places,' he said gently. 'Maybe you're looking for the wrong thing.'

'You don't understand. And I can't explain it. I know what I need,' she insisted.

'Do you?'

'Daniel, you're missing the point,' she told him doggedly. 'The way I grew up, the places I lived helped me learn a lot, about myself and about my needs.'

'What about love, Markie? What did you learn about that?'

'I learned that it's a very precious thing,' she answered quietly. 'And that it comes first from inside yourself.'

His eyes shadowed. 'That's quite a lesson for a six-year-old.'

Markie smiled slightly. 'It made me a stronger seven-year-old.'

'What else did you learn in those thirteen foster homes, Markie?'

'I learned about stength and individuality and talent——'

'What about fun and laughter and touching?' he asked quietly, eyes shadowed. Soundlessly, he moved closer, and lifted one hand to her. 'What did you learn about touching, Markie?'

She blinked, arrested by his sudden proximity.

His finger traced her delicate jaw and his silver eyes followed the motion. 'Did you learn that there are different kinds of touching?'

She managed a small shake of her head.

'I didn't think so,' he continued, exploring the delicate cleft in her chin. 'But there are, you know, all different kinds. There's the way your family might touch you. Perhaps Griff——?'

Markie's eyes softened involuntarily as she recalled those long-ago days when she had tagged after Griff. He had touched her: friendly, as he ruffled her hair, concerned, as he picked her up from a tumble, comforting, as he explained that they were going to be separated. Family touches. . .

'Brother touches. . .' She murmured, understanding. 'I liked that.'

Daniel smiled quietly. 'But it's different from the way friends touch. Earlier, did you like that?'

She searched his eyes before admitting softly, 'I don't know. It wasn't like Griff.'

'What was it like?'

She shook her head uncertainly. 'I don't know. I guess it was like—friends?'

'You sound unsure.'

'Daniel,' she sighed, 'I have friends all over the country, people I've met in the last six years whom I like and respect. But I never felt the same with them as I do with you. I never wanted to touch them. I never noticed if they touched me. I don't understand it.'

'Do you want to understand it?'

Markie didn't answer.

'We could—explore it further,' he suggested softly.

Disquiet flared in her eyes and Daniel read it easily. 'I don't think——'

'Why, just in the "friends" category alone, there must be a thousand different kinds of touches;' he pressed on lightly, trying to calm her fears. 'Like before, when we were just—playing around. That would be different from when you burned the toast or used all the hot water.'

Markie laughed, relaxing. 'I'm glad we're friends, Daniel.'

He sighed silently and released her very carefully. 'I'm glad we are too, Markie.'

* * *

Markie sat up in bed abruptly, tears raining silently down her cheeks. The room was dark; the clock on the nightstand showed a few minutes past midnight.

It was the nightmare that had awakened her, she realised vaguely. More memory than nightmare, she admitted silently. A little girl with long dark hair and tears in her eyes, trying to understand why the closest thing she had ever had to family was leaving her. Trying to understand why she was alone again. . .

Hurriedly she pushed the blankets away, abandoning the bed in hopes of leaving the dream behind. Maybe some tea would help, she thought doubtfully, reaching for the robe Daniel had given her that first night.

Thanks to thick insulation and sound construction, the bedroom was almost soundproof. Once the door was closed, noise rarely penetrated the room. But now, as Markie opened the door into the hallway, she heard the melody floating down from the loft and realised that Daniel was still working.

It wasn't tea she needed, she thought as she slipped into the hallway. It was the knowledge, however fleeting, that she wasn't alone. Most of the time it didn't bother her, the feeling of isolation and loneliness. She had, after all, experienced that emotion all her life and had long ago made peace with it. But occasionally she woke up in the dark, crying tears that never saw the light of day, needing to know that there was something beyond the darkness. Usually, the only comfort she found was in the thought of her search. Tonight she discovered something more concrete. Tonight there was Daniel.

Soundlessly she moved into the living area and curled up on the lounger. Here the music from the piano was stronger and she could even hear the faint rumble of Daniel's voice as he struggled with a chord or lyric. An involuntary smile tilted her mouth. It was chilly in the room, but she was too sleepy suddenly to go for a blanket. Besides, listening to the distant sound of Daniel's music, she felt a little warmer. . .

Over an hour later, Daniel was finally satisfied with the song he was writing. And almost tired enough, he thought irritably, to fall asleep without thoughts of Markie interrupting. He rose from the bench and stretched hugely.

She had been with him for a week now. By coincidence, that was the exact length of time since he had last been in possession of his peace of mind. Or any piece of mind, he thought ironically. Either description would be accurate. When he had met Markie, both had deserted him.

She unsettled him, he thought crossly, descending the stairs. She confused him and delighted him and aroused him. Was it simply that he had been alone too long? He had spent the last six months writing songs and void of companionship, but he had done the same for years now and never had such a reaction. No, it was Markie's fault. She was the one who had invaded his life and turned it upside-down. She was the one who had brought colour into his calm grey world. She was——

Asleep on the lounger. Daniel halted in his tracks and stared at her huddled form. Why wasn't she in bed? he wondered worriedly, crossing to her side. She was curled up tightly in defence of the cold, with no blanket or pillow for comfort. She wore his robe, which was miles too big for her, and looked lost and vulnerable and soft.

Daniel went down on his haunches beside the lounger. Soft. God, yes, she was soft. In sleep, she was as helpless and as needy as a child. Such a contradiction, he thought gently, because Markie was as strong and determined a woman as he had ever known. Courageous, intelligent, funny, kind, he listed mentally. And yet there was a shadow of sadness in her that she tried and never quite succeeded in hiding. He wondered if it would ever fade, even when she found the home she sought.

Involuntarily his hand lifted and one finger lightly traced her lips.

'Daniel?' Her voice was husky, more asleep than awake.

He didn't answer, merely dropping his hand and waiting for her to be reclaimed by sleep. When she had settled again, he stood and scooped her into his arms, carrying her back to her bedroom.

The blankets were scattered, he noted, as if she had slept restlessly. He eased her on to the mattress and smoothed the blankets over her. She murmured restlessly at the loss of his warmth, then quieted.

In the fall of moonlight, Daniel studied her for a long time, curiously disturbed, before he sighed and slipped from the room.

CHAPTER SEVEN

THE next morning, a warm, soft breeze moved in and the snow began to melt. Markie sat at the kitchen table and stared disconsolately out of the window. She should be relieved. Soon she would be free to continue her search. Instead she felt bereft, as if something vital were being taken from her.

As she stuggled to come to terms with the confusion, Daniel shambled in. His eyes were still half closed with sleep and he reached blindly for the coffee-pot.

'Morning,' he offered grumpily.

Markie barely suppressed a smile. After eight days, she was used to Daniel's morning face. At the best of times, he didn't greet the day happily. And last night, she remembered, he had been up late writing songs. . .and carrying her to bed. When she had woken up this morning in her room, she knew that he was responsible.

As she watched an icicle slowly melt outside the window, she realised that there would be no more mornings, no more nights with Daniel.

'Good morning.'

Daniel had taken two sips of the bracing brew before he realised that Markie was unusually silent. She had never been a soothing morning companion, always bright and wide awake at dawn's first light. 'What's wrong?'

'Nothing,' she answered in true feminine fashion.

He eyed her disbelievingly and waited.

'The snow's melting,' she remarked at last, striving for a casual tone.

He shifted to look out of the window, narrowing his eyes against the bright glare. It was melting, he thought bleakly. Soon it would be gone, and with it, Markie. 'It's a slow process,' he cautioned. 'It could take another few days before the roads are clear enough, even for a four-wheel-drive vehicle.'

For a second, a flickering fraction of time, Markie's mask of indifference cracked and raw emotion spilled from her eyes. And then it was gone.

It had been such a fleeting revelation, Daniel thought in frustration. Like a door opening, then quickly slamming shut again, before he had the chance to examine what had been exposed.

'I guess I'll be out of your way soon,' she remarked evenly. 'You'll have your solitude back and I'll have my——'

'Your what?' he challenged harshly.

When she didn't answer, he decided to gamble on the emotion she had so briefly revealed.

'You could stay,' he offered abruptly.

'Stay?' she echoed incredulously.

'Why not?' His tone was challenging. 'There's no one waiting for you. You like it here. You do like my home, don't you, Markie?'

She nodded wordlessly. Yes, she liked his home. For her, it was like a bright, warm oasis, a sweet shelter. Not the wood and bricks and glass, but. . . Daniel. Markie flinched visibly. Daniel was the attraction, the warmth, the shelter.

'And you have a book to finish,' he persisted, overriding her silence. 'You could do that here.'

'But that could take——' Weeks, she realised faintly. Months. 'A long time.'

'I'm not going anywhere.'

'But winter's gone,' she protested. 'Don't you have to record your songs and work on your next release?'

'I don't have to do anything,' he returned quietly. 'Besides, my songs aren't finished yet. I've been working on—something else.'

She looked at him curiously, but didn't ask for details. 'Why would you want me to stay?'

'Maybe I've gotten used to having you around,' he answered gruffly, looking away.

'I don't think——'

'We're friends, aren't we?' he broke in across her refusal. 'Friends don't just walk out when the opportunity arises.'

Markie studied him with pained perception. 'You've been lonely, haven't you?'

'I'd be lonely,' he answered carefully, 'if you left.'

The words hurt as they cut at her heart. He would be lonely, and so would she. No more late-night talks or drifting music. No more grumpy mornings or shared laughter. She couldn't let go of that, not yet.

'You'd be sacrificing your solitude.'

Daniel reached for her hand and held it tightly. 'That's my choice to make. And yours. You're not trapped here any more. Make a choice.'

He was wrong, she thought gravely. There was no choice, only need. And she needed. . . Once it had been so simple. Before Daniel, it had been so clear. Now she couldn't see past the friendship and the warmth and the intimacy he offered.

'I'll stay,' she told him quietly, searching his eyes. 'For a while.'

He framed her face between his hands, reading the confusion and desire there. His eyes holding hers, he slowly lowered his mouth until it touched hers, a kiss of comfort and warmth.

Markie sat perfectly still, absorbing the sensation of Daniel's lips on her own. With his touch came the same feeling of shelter that his presence brought, only it was deeper, warmer, more intimate. She felt it in her head and in her heart. She sighed against his mouth and closed her eyes.

She didn't see the frown that drew Daniel's brows together, or the shadow of uncertainty that darkened his eyes. Carefully, he pulled away, watching as her eyes fluttered open.

Her tongue swept delicately against ther lips, picking up his taste. She wasn't aware of the action, but Daniel was, and he swallowed tightly.

'I liked that,' she murmured simply, searching his eyes.

'So did I.'

'I've never kissed a friend before, temporary or otherwise.'

He held her gaze cautiously. 'Maybe we should find out where this could lead.'

Markie drew away slightly, just as cautious. 'Daniel, in the past eight days we've gone from rivals to strangers to friends. Things are happening too fast. I'm not ready for anything else.'

'I'm not asking you to let go of the friendship, Markie. I'm just asking you to hold on for a while longer. Is that too much?'

She was torn between confusion and painful honesty. 'I can't promise that I'll stay long enough to finish the book,' she warned him carefully.

He nodded, just once. 'Then stay, Markie. . .until you can't.'

Threads of intimacy wove themselves into the pattern of their days. Daniel and Markie spent more time together than they ever had before, sneaking stealthy moments away from work to talk or hike or simply be silent.

Oddly, though they spent less time on their professional pursuits, both noticed an increased productivity, a higher quality of output. Daniel's music was purer, more lyrical; Markie's book was cleaner, more poetic.

And when they were together, during meals or the long, quiet hours of the evening, they talked as they never had before. It was as if, with the conscious choice to be together, a barrier had been lifted. Caution was gone, distance breached. The friendship deepened into intimacy and beyond as the weeks passed.

Spring took a firm hold on Colorado, brightening the land with emerald grass and jewelled flowers. Only at the highest elevations did the snow continue. At Daniel's home, warmer breezes nourished the land and gave life to the plants.

The wild flowers were in full bloom, a riot of joyous colour. Markie was in bloom as well.

They talked about everything. Markie learned about the things Daniel cared most about: his home, his sense of strength and purpose, the environment. In turn, she shared bits and pieces of her life, the good times and the bad.

It was a kind of friendship that she had never before envisaged, more and less than she expected. More, because the emotional closeness was overwhelming. And less, because she sometimes wondered about an equal physical closeness.

She found herself watching Daniel as he moved, a curious ache catching at her heart. She was profoundly aware of the hard length of his thighs and the intimidating breadth of his shoulders. His masculine strength made her conscious of her own femininity in a way she delighted in exploring.

When she realised that what she felt for him was more than friendship, that it combined a searing physical awareness with emotional need, equal parts of concern and respect and tenderness, she accepted the truth.

Markie Smith, whose knowledge of love was limited to second-hand observation, was falling in love. And she was terrified.

'Tell me about your first date.'

Markie met his gaze mildly, a slight smile on her mouth. She was becoming accustomed to Daniel's impulsive questions about her past. He made it easy for her to share the things she didn't know how to broach, easy to open herself to him. Now she stretched to ease muscles that had cramped from the hours spent lying here on the floor by the fireplace and answered, 'That's easy enough. I've never been on a date.'

He stared at her incredulously. 'Never been on a date? Why?'

She shrugged. 'Remember how I grew up, Daniel. I was always the new kid in school, the outsider. The only peace or permanence I ever found came from reading, and that's a pretty solitary occupation.'

Truthfully, she had never missed the interaction with the opposite sex, never missed the awkward moments or shattering uncertainties. Until now.

'Were the people in the foster programme very strict?' he asked.

'Strict?' She considered that uneasily. 'I wouldn't say that. I just had other things on my mind.'

'Go on a date with me.'

She blinked, just once, then burst out, 'A date? Why in the world would you want to go on a date with me?'

He didn't smile. 'Because I want to be your first. . .' The hesitation was deliberate, Markie knew that. Yet even with that knowledge she couldn't prevent the shattering image that raced through her mind or the tremor that slipped through her limbs. Daniel noted the reaction with satisfaction, and finished softly, '. . .date.'

She drew a steadying breath and tried to marshal her unruly imagination. 'When?'

'I was thinking about tomorrow night.'

Her eyes narrowed. 'Tomorrow night?'

'You have a scheduling conflict?' Daniel suggested drily.

'Tomorrow night,' she echoed incredulously. 'What did you have in mind? A quick jaunt to the newest play on Broadway, and dinner at Sardi's?'

'I'm planning something a little closer to home,' he explained gently. 'I'll take care of arranging our evening. Is it a date?'

'No.'

He smiled as if he hadn't heard the flat denial. 'Good. I'll pick you up at seven o'clock.'

'Pick me up?' she questioned, somewhat dazed by his blatant tactics.

'At your door,' he explained. 'Like the gentleman that I am.'

Markie responded with a rather unladylike sound. 'Daniel——'

'Formal attire,' he continued breezily.

'Which means?' she prompted, aware that he was intimately familiar with every item in her meagre wardrobe.

'Socks required.'

'Ah. Formal, indeed?' Markie couldn't prevent a smile. It was ludicrous, really. There was no reason for the panic that had assailed her at Daniel's innocent request for a date. It was, without a doubt, a continuation of their efforts to learn more about each other. And that prospect was something she was unable to resist. 'Very well, Mr Reed, it's a date.'

They shook hands solemnly, and Markie didn't see the triumph beneath the silver depths of Daniel's eyes.

At precisely seven o'clock the following evening, Daniel knocked on Markie's bedroom door. She ran suddenly damp palms down the sides of her jeans and laughed breathlessly.

She was nervous. It was ridiculous. She had spent most of the day with Daniel, as she had since her decision to stay. They had parted only two hours ago to prepare for their coming date, with a word from Daniel about 'arrangements' to be made. For the last hour she had been teased with a wonderful aroma drifting from the kitchen and the sound of Daniel's mysterious arrangements. It was time for her first date to begin.

She drew a calming breath and opened the bedroom door.

Daniel studied her closely without appearing to do so. She was wearing a large shirt that looked suspiciously like his own tucked into the waistband of her best jeans. The tie knotted loosely around her neck was definitely his own, he thought in amusement. Formal attire. Her dark hair was as unruly as ever, although it hinted at her attempt and failure to tame it. Her face was scrubbed clean, pure ivory with no trace of make-up, and her scent was that which Daniel knew he would always associate with wild flowers.

He took all this in within the space of seconds. In front of him was the woman he had lived with for the last few weeks, and he thought quite helplessly that she was lovely.

'This is for you.' He handed her the single snowflower

he had picked and smiled gently. Curiously, he witnessed the faint tremor in her answering smile.

'Daniel,' she sighed his name, allowing one finger to delicately trace a petal. 'Thank you!'

'It's not a bouquet of roses.'

'No, it's not,' she agreed. 'It's much better.'

'I only picked one,' he continued a little awkwardly. 'Wild flowers should be allowed to grow free, but I couldn't resist giving you this.' He reached to touch the flower and felt her fingers instead. Cautiously he drew away. 'It reminds me of you.'

'Me?'

'It's so pretty,' he explained whimsically. 'And it looks so delicate. But in reality, it's strong enough to survive almost anything. That's you, isn't it?'

Markie tried to speak, but no words emerged. Pretty? Did he really think she was pretty? And, more important, did he really understand the strength that she had fought so hard to build within herself?

Daniel saw the questions she couldn't voice and sighed silently. Somehow he had to make her believe that he understood and accepted her as she was. If only she would give him the chance.

Markie fingered her tie nervously. 'I—er—just found this. . .lying around.'

Daniel nodded solemnly. 'It goes well with the shirt.'

She had the grace to flush, but a mischievous smile tugged at her lips. 'Thank you. You did say formal attire.'

'Indeed. If you're ready, Markie, I've made dinner reservations for seven-fifteen.' Gallantly he offered his arm.

Markie suppressed a smile and replied with equal formality. 'Yes, Daniel, I'm ready.'

They stepped from the room. Daniel watched as she meticulously closed her bedroom door.

'Not going to lock it?' he chided facetiously.

'This is a very low crime area,' she answered solemnly. 'I've never had a break-in.'

And that, he thought quite soberly, was probably true. As far as he could tell, no one had ever breached Markie's personal security.

'You can't be too casual about these things,' he continued in the same vein. 'I live quite near here and was recently confronted with a trespasser.'

Markie wrinkled her nose and pinched his arm. 'Oh?'

'Bold as brass,' he told her cheerfully. 'Found a place for herself among the wild flowers and settled in.'

'Without asking permission?'

'Wild flowers don't ask permission.'

'Your trespasser did.'

Daniel stopped to run a gentle finger down her cheek, his eyes holding hers. 'She no more needed permission than the wild flowers did. I understand that now.'

Markie, totally aware of his caress, steeled herself against its effects. 'The whole incident sounds like a false alarm.'

He dropped his hand. 'Perhaps you're right. Well, here we are.'

She blinked, freed from the power of his touch. Her eyes left his face to focus in the direction he indicated. They stood at the entrance of the dining-room, but she had been so involved in their conversation that she hadn't noticed.

The room had been transformed from the familiar and somewhat haphazard work area she was used to into a corner of quiet elegance. The table was beautifully arranged with china and crystal, two settings close together. Four candles provided a gentle light that was reflected and magnified in the glassware. The room radiated an ambience of soft intimacy, a serenity that she found deeply appealing.

'Daniel,' she turned to him, her eyes bright, 'it's perfect!'

He smiled, pleased. 'I selected this place especially for our first date. It's very casual. We can sit any place we want.'

She nodded solemnly. 'How about this table?'

Daniel grinned approvingly. 'Excellent choice.' With manners that were deeply ingrained, he pulled out Markie's chair and seated her.

She carefully placed the snowflower beside her plate before lifting her eyes to Daniel. The candlelight reflected there as well, and she felt that warmth as if the flames were directly on her skin.

'Wine?'

'Wine?' she repeated, somewhat dazed by the heat building inside her. Trying to deal with this, she only absently noted the bottle he held. 'Daniel, have you been holding out on me?'

'It's only the one bottle.'

'And what else?' she wondered aloud.

He stiffened imperceptibly. 'You really want to know?'

Markie decided, quite suddenly, that she did. 'Yes.'

'Ask me after dinner.'

'Will you tell me?'

His eyes went cautious. 'Will you ask me?'

She tore her eyes from his face and listened to the silence that followed. She would ask him, but she wondered if she was ready for the answer.

Daniel poured the wine and lifted his glass. 'To our first date, Markie.'

She noted his use of the phrase 'first date', as though

he intended that there should be others, but she didn't question it. In honesty, she admitted that she wished it could be so, and tonight wishing was enough. So tonight she accepted the toast. . .and wished.

Dinner was excellent. Although limited by the absence of fresh vegetables, Daniel had managed to prepare a meal considerably superior to their standard fare. Braised chicken breasts in wine sauce were accompanied by roasted new potatoes and asparagus tips. Markie ate every bite on her plate and complimented him lavishly.

If the accompanying conversation was more familiar than that of a couple on their first date, if the silences were more comfortable and the words more meaningful, neither objected. Beneath it all they carried on a silent conversation, filled with a depth of understanding that only came from living together day after day in deepening intimacy.

In a moment of silence, Markie watched melted wax trail down the side of one candle and wondered how it was possible to feel so comfortable with Daniel, yet ache at the same time.

'Finished?'

She drew her eyes from the flame and focused on him. 'Yes,' she agreed softly. 'Let me help you clear up.'

Daniel covered her hand with his own to stop her from rising. 'Leave it for the hired help.'

She looked around regretfully. 'Not a bus-boy in sight.'

He tightened his hold and pulled her to her feet beside him. 'Probably waiting for us to leave the table—the mark of excellent service.'

Markie smiled into his eyes. 'All right. We've had dinner. What comes next?'

'Whatever you want.'

Her face softened with pleasure. 'Music?'

Daniel couldn't prevent his fingers from lifting to trace the line of her jaw. 'You want me to play?'

'Please.' He hadn't played for her since that first day. Every day she heard fragments of the melodies he created, but he had never offered her more. Markie, intensely private, had never asked for more. Now, tonight, it seemed right that she should.

'I'll play for you,' he conceded.

She picked up her flower and brushed the petals absently against her lips as Daniel extinguished the candles' flames. When the room was in shadow, he took her hand, and they climbed the stairs to the music-room together.

Once there, he settled behind the piano and Markie took the place she had claimed as her own. Carefully she laid the snowflower aside so that her hands could rest flat against the gleaming wood.

'What should I play?' he asked.

'The songs you've been working on these last few weeks?' she prompted hopefully.

Daniel shook his head. 'No, Markie. Something else.'

She was aware of a deep reluctance in his tone, a silent rejection that hurt more than it should have. So he didn't want to share those songs with her, she chided herself silently. There were things that she had not shared— could not share—with Daniel, as well. She had no right to ask from him things that she herself was unwilling to give. No right to want.

'Markie——'

She heard the concern in his tone and knew that he must have seen what she couldn't hide. It wasn't fair, she told herself fiercely, that she should cause him concern. It wasn't fair that something inside her delighted to know that she could.

'It's all right, Daniel,' she dismissed gently. 'I understand an artist's reluctance to share an unfinished work. I'm the same way about my novels, honestly. Play anything. Play your favourite songs.'

She blanked the hurt from her face and met his eyes encouragingly. She withstood his careful perusal and only smiled. 'Please, Daniel. Play.'

Daniel drew his eyes away, unsatisfied with what he had found in her, yet uncertain how to proceed. He couldn't give her the songs that she had asked for, and he couldn't tell her why. Instead, he determined, he would give her another part of himself. Maybe it would be enough. His fingers lifted to the keys, and he coaxed the music he sought.

He played until the muscles in his arms protested against the stiff position and his fingers cramped. Classical and jazz pieces were threaded through with some of his own work, creating a tapestry of beauty.

Markie felt every note as it left his fingers and filtered through the strings and wood beneath her hands. When he stopped after the final, haunting melody, she felt the loss of her music as intensely as she had felt its power.

'Daniel, that was beautiful,' she told him sincerely. 'What talent you have!'

'Talent demands a price,' he said wryly, flexing his fingers painfully as he rose from the bench.

She studied him, a haunting question shadowing her eyes. 'Is it worth it?'

'Oh, yes,' he nodded, moving to stand before her. 'The beauty and the satisfaction more than make up for the pain.'

Without volition, she reached for his hands, her fingers moving soothingly over his own. 'Wouldn't it be wonderful,' she mused a little distantly, 'if everything were like that?'

Daniel's fingers twisted to capture hers and only then did she become aware that she had reached for him. 'What makes you think it isn't, Markie?'

She looked away. 'Experience,' she answered evenly. 'Sometimes there's no beauty, no satisfaction. Just pain.'

'You're thinking of the foster homes.'

With a sudden, almost unbearable ache, Markie knew that Daniel was wrong. She was thinking of her search, of all the years she had travelled alone and lonely, looking for something she never found, hungry for something she had never tasted. Until Daniel. When he had taken her into his home, offered his friendship, listened to her and held her even when she tried to back away, she had finally caught a glimpse of that beauty. She wanted more. God, she wanted everything! Tonight she was afraid she was going to ask for it. And she was afraid of what that asking would rob her of.

Daniel tensed suddenly, as though he had somehow read the emotions that shook her. 'Ask me,' he urged with shattering intensity. 'Markie, *ask me!*'

She could no more stop the words than she could stop her next breath. 'Earlier, you said I should ask you about the things you've been hiding from me——' She broke off, struggling to control her trembling tone. 'Daniel, is any part of it. . .satisfaction and beauty?'

He held her eyes and traced her brow with one long finger. 'Are you really ready to find out?'

Something—confusion, need—flickered on her face. 'Ready? I don't know. But I think I *need* to find out.'

Daniel measured her in silence, part hesitation, part fire. Finally, quietly, his hand cupped her jaw and his mouth lowered to hers.

Their gazes held, unblinking, until the first breath of contact, then closed on the resulting wave of sensation. His lips brushed hers once, twice, before he pulled back.

Markie's eyes opened slowly, and glimmered with questions. A slight crease furrowed her forehead and echoed the confusion.

'Daniel——?'

'I've wanted to kiss you for—a long time.' He searched her face. 'I think you've wanted it too.'

'Beauty, Daniel,' she agreed tacitly. 'But where is the satisfaction?'

Breath suspended deep in his chest, he answered carefully, 'In the beauty. In the friendship. In. . .this.'

He moved again to take her lips, but the taking was different this time. In one small corner of her mind, Markie acknowledged and revelled in that difference.

His arms took her as well, pulling her into an over-whelming embrace. His hands took her, caressing with drugging sweeps through her tousled hair to her flaring hips. His body took her, warm and growing warmer, urging hers to melt against him. And his need took her from the intimacy of the music-room on that deserted mountain-top to an intimacy she had never known and a place she had never dreamed of.

Softly his mouth slanted over hers, refining angle and depth. Her lips parted instinctively, inviting a sweeter exploration. Daniel's tongue moistened her bottom lip with tender precision, then moved beyond to greater softness.

Markie sighed and felt him tremble, and a shadow of wonder danced in her heart. She had never been so physically close to another human being. One of the legacies of the foster-care system was the distance, physcial and emotional, she now maintained between herself and others.

Daniel had been stealthily eroding the emotional distance over the last weeks, chipping off small and large pieces with every moment of shared laughter, every hour of silence and companionship, every day of friendship. Now he challenged the physical aspect of that isolation, and Markie was responding like a desert to rain, awakening to life and blooming with colour.

Because the sensation of embers from ashes was so enticing, she pressed closer to the source of the flame and was warmed.

Carefully, Daniel eased her to the floor before the fireplace, urging thir bodies into deeper intimacy. His lips moved across her face, caressing her from temple to chin to jaw, delighting in the ivory purity of her skin.

His voice husky with passion, he whispered, 'The music, Markie. Do you hear the music?'

The music he heard resulted from the exquisite merging of two bodies playing on one another, the lyrical touch of hands and mouth and flesh, the building rhythm of heartbeats and passions.

Markie heard the music and was swept away by its power. 'Beautiful. . .'

Daniel drew back, just inches, to study her with fierce intentness. 'Beautiful,' he agreed softly.

When he nudged the first button of her shirt unfastened, a fraction of sanity broke through the hazy hunger clouding her mind.

'Daniel, what——?'

Swiftly his mouth claimed hers, silencing the question, defusing the concern. Another button was undone, and then another, until he could slip one hand beneath the material and find the sweet curve of her breast.

Markie flinched, not from pain but from the sensation of fire that met his touch. Daniel smoothed the tender rise with callused fingers until he found the hardening peak. As he had taken her mouth, he took her breast; softly, once, twice.

She shivered and sighed. 'Daniel, I can't think when you. . .do that.'

'I'm thinking,' he promised against her lips, parting her shirt completely.

'What—are you thinking?' she asked, vibrantly aware of his mouth as he began a warm, rough trek down her body.

'I'm thinking about passion.' He nibbled at her collarbone, then soothed the small hurt with his tongue. 'And about weeks of needing.' His chest brushed enticingly over her breasts, the material of his shirt rough and somehow arousing against her sensitive flesh. 'I'm thinking about how much it hurts to come to life, how painful a rainbow can be to eyes used to grey.'

'I don't understand,' she protested, plaintive because she wanted to understand everything about him.

'Maybe it's best if you don't. I want you to understand pleasure, Markie. Let me worry about the rest.'

For a moment, a moment when Markie arched helplessly against him, the words didn't register. His mouth had reached her breast and she was lost in that pleasure he wanted for and brought to her. But like the persistent fall of water, his words impressed themselves on her mind. Understanding came, swift and painful.

She had made a physical decision, she realised, helped along by Daniel's expert lovemaking. But she had made no intellectual decision, no emotional one. And he was asking her not to. Pleasure, he said, for her. Commit her body, but not her mind. Don't ask, don't know his mind, the needs neither body could convey. Days ago, he had said something so different, and she had taken those words to heart and soul.

Now he was taking her, she realised belatedly, when they should be taking each other. She should be walking by his side, making the choice, taking the chance.

The chance. . .

'Stop!' she cried with sudden panic, realising how willing she had been to give up her responsibilities.

He almost ignored her. He almost kissed her in an attempt to silence the protest. He almost carried her to his room, to his bed, where he needed her so badly. But then he looked into her eyes, and read the panic there. Nothing could override that.

Her voice was husky with arousal, but determined. Daniel's entire body tensed and stilled. Markie felt the frustration in every inch of muscle and sinew against her, and felt the echo in her own yearning body. Quite helplessly, she wondered how firm a grip either of them had on control.

'You want me.' His voice dared denial.

'Yes. *Here*,' she agreed, covering his hand at her breast and pressing it hard so they could both feel her heartbeat. 'What about——?'

'The decision has been made.' If the words were arrogant, it was something he couldn't control. In his head, in his gut, he knew it to be true.

'Not by me. Not yet.'

He held her eyes, willing her with fire and frustration to relent. She met the challenge directly and without words. Endless minutes passed as they battled silently, measuring wills and needs. At last Daniel rolled away with a sound caught somewhere between a sigh and a groan.

Markie sat up slowly and buttoned her shirt with unsteady fingers. Her eyes never left him, and her skin felt as if he had never left her. She could still feel his fingers and his lips and his tongue on her flesh.

'Daniel.'

He swallowed and turned to face her.

'I can't come to you like this: physically aroused and

emotionally numbed. I don't think you want me that way. And what about friendship?'

'You want me,' he gritted in a harsh and driven tone.

She sighed despairingly. 'Daniel.'

'I want you.'

Markie could deny neither statement. But somehow she had to make him understand why she had to walk away. Very aware of his fierce regard, she rose to her feet. 'Maybe, when I understand what goes with the physcial need, I'll be ready for that wanting.' Her eyes turned sombre as she searched for words. 'I think you were wrong, Daniel. I think the satisfaction lies in understanding the beauty, not in the beauty itself. I want that, but I want it to be right.'

He watched in silence as she crossed the room and descended the stairs, wishing he could make it right for her. Knowing that only she could do that.

On the gleaming satinwood of the piano, the snow-flower beckoned in the moonlight.

CHAPTER EIGHT

HOURS later, Markie made her decision—made it the way she had to, with her heart *and* her mind. In doing so, she opened the door of the cage she had built for herself over long, lonely years. Poised on the brink, she knew that she must take the first step. Determination held like a shield and a spur inside her, she headed for Daniel's room. The hallway was dark, but her eyes had adjusted during the long hours spent alone in her room, thinking of what was to come, and why.

She found the doorknob easily, and entered the room without a sound. Somehow she knew Daniel wouldn't be sleeping. She was sure that their earlier encounter haunted him as it haunted her. She had seen it in his eyes as she had taken that first small step away.

In fact, his bed was unoccupied, and her eyes focused on it blankly. He wasn't there. Through all the hours she had spent girding herself for this confrontation, she had imagined every possibility but this.

Perhaps the music-room. . . She was just turning away when a soft sound caught her attention. Daniel, she thought, heart pounding. Across the darkness of the room, her gaze found him. He was sprawled in one of the chairs in the sitting area by the windows. In the faint filter of moonlight, he looked hard and brooding and desperately uncomfortable. With his back towards the door, he was unaware of her presence.

Markie watched as he shifted restlessly, his eyes fixed unseeingly through the windows. He had thrown the curtains open, leaving nothing to block the rays of the moon.

The fragile light touched the room with delicate fingers, softening the hard contours of furniture and walls. But it did not soften him. Instead, it seemed to highlight his face more starkly, picking out a recklessness and anguish and need that Markie had never seen in him before. That he had never let her see.

It was that need, and her own, that drove her forward—irrevocably forward.

'Daniel.'

His name was a sigh, a whisper as soft as moonlight and as inevitable. Moving to stand before him, she saw his eyes close at the sound, saw his jaw tense before he spoke.

'You should be asleep, Markie. It's past midnight.'

She lowered herself to the table before him, knee to knee, face to face. 'You're not sleeping,' she pointed out gently.

He shrugged dismissively. 'I'm not tired.'

Her eyes lingered on his face. 'It was a long day.'

'It was a hell of a day,' Daniel agreed roughly, unable to prevent his eyes from finding hers. 'Look, Markie, if you're worried about what happened earlier——'

'I'm not.'

'—don't.' He didn't seem to hear her soft disclaimer. 'You made it clear that that wasn't what you wanted from me, and I swear I won't pressure you. I value our friendship too much to risk losing it over. . .sex.'

'It wasn't what I wanted.'

He turned his head. 'Right. So let's just forget it.'

'I was close to being swept away by the emotions you aroused in me tonight. Emotions I didn't even know I was capable of feeling,' she told him evenly, determined to make him understand. 'Passion, desire, hunger so real, Daniel, that it was like a physical pain inside me.'

'You pulled away,' he reminded her roughly. 'You ran.'

'I told you why.'

'No. You told me why you should have *stayed*, Markie. You wanted me. I—wanted you,' he admitted harshly. 'There was no reason to run.'

'There was,' she insisted. 'You were overwhelming me with that wanting, mine and yours. I wanted to give in. . .but I kept remembering what you said the other day. And I couldn't come to you that way.'

Daniel grimaced in the darkness. 'It couldn't have been that overwhelming for you if you were able to think about something other than what we were doing to each other.'

She tilted her head. 'Couldn't you think, Daniel?'

His mouth twisted with self-derision. 'Think? Hell, Markie. I couldn't even remember to breathe!'

She reached for his hand and held it firmly between her own, despite his instinctive, abortive effort to pull away. 'I remembered what you said, about romance being a mutual decision. Not being swept away blind, but choosing to go that way, eyes open. I didn't want you to be responsible for what happened. I wanted us to be responsible. That's why I left, Daniel. I needed to be sure it was what I wanted.' She searched his face for understanding, then admitted softly, 'That's why I came back.'

His eyes narrowed, and his hand tightened almost painfully on her own. 'And are you sure?'

'Oh, yes,' she smiled. 'I'm sure I want you, Daniel Reed. With my heart and my head.'

Oddly, he didn't move to take her into his arms.

Instead, he went curiously still, like a man who has looked down to find himself on the edge of a precipice.

'Why?' One syllable, but he barely managed it at all.

'Why?' Markie repeated whimsically, aware of a soft warmth building inside her. 'Maybe because the moon is full, and it's shining on the wild flowers.'

'Markie.' His fingers tightened warningly.

She smiled at the implicit threat and eased herself from the table. Now on her knees before him, she raised her free hand to his face, stroking softly. 'Maybe because it's spring, or perhaps because it's Tuesday.'

He turned his lips against her palm, allowing her soft skin to muffle his rusty rejoinder. 'It's Wednesday.'

She laughed, then sobered slowly. 'Maybe because you seem to fit me so well, Daniel. Because you understand how lonely I've been. Because when you hold me in your arms, I feel——'

'Feel what?' The demand was urgent, as urgent as the hands that closed over her shoulders to pull her on to the chair with him, settling her carefully on his lap. 'What do you feel in my arms, sweetheart?'

Markie leaned forward, her lips moving softly over his face in the moonlight. 'It isn't friendship,' she mused hesitantly against his brow. 'But. . .it is.'

Daniel sighed and wrapped his arms more tightly around her.

'It isn't safety,' she murmured against his jaw. 'But. . .it is.'

'Oh, sweet lord!'

'It isn't comfort, or security, or recognition,' she finished, her lips moving against his own. 'But. . .it is.'

She deepened the kiss with newly discovered skill, and drew him along effortlessly. They met in hunger and silence, lips parted, bodies close. Finally, Daniel drew away.

'Do you——' He broke off roughly as her hands flattened against his chest. 'Do you have any better idea of what it is you feel now, Markie?'

She met his eyes, suddenly troubled. It wasn't a casual question he asked her. There was a sombreness in him, a waiting. But Markie didn't know what he was waiting for. At that precise moment, she realised, she didn't know much of anything. Only need, and desire. And Daniel, always Daniel.

'What do you want me to say, Daniel?'

Something in his eyes, a light that had burned too briefly, flickered out. 'Only the truth, Markie. And you've given me that, haven't you?'

'Yes.' Her eyes clouded. 'Is it enough?'

He rested his head against the back of the chair and stared past her out the windows. 'Yes,' he managed at length. 'It's enough.'

Markie studied him warily from her perch on his lap. 'Daniel, it occurs to me that the purpose of my grand gesture hasn't really been served.'

'In what way?'

'I was so concerned that whatever happened betwen us be mutual,' she told him, chagrined. 'And I spent hours examining my feelings, my needs until the decision was made. I didn't even stop to think that you might not want this.'

'Not want this?' he repeated incredulously, focusing sharply on her once again. 'Are you crazy?'

She blinked. 'I don't think so.'

'Think again,' he advised ironically. 'Markie, you're sitting on my lap. That position should make it abundantly obvious that I want this.'

Markie flushed, but persisted. It was so terribly important that they both be certain. 'But do you *choose* to want it, Daniel? It's not just—passion, is it?'

He studied her intently. 'Do you want more?'

'I want you to decide this with your mind, not your body. I need you to want me here——' she touched his temple lightly '—as well as here.' Her hand settled on his chest.

'Markie, I want you.' His hand closed on hers, holding it against him. 'And I chose to want you. Is that what you needed to hear?'

'Like you, I only needed the truth.' Her eyes softened. 'I want to make love with you, Daniel. Always with you.'

He held her gaze for one long, pounding minute, then carefully eased her from his lap. When they were on their feet, standing side by side, he tangled his fingers between hers.

'Will you come to bed with me?'

Markie's heart tightened. She understood what he was doing. It would have been so easy, so. . .scenic for him to sweep her into his arms and carry to his bed. Instead, he was inviting her to walk at his side, hand in hand, heart to heart.

'Yes.'

They walked without speaking and at the side of the bed maintained that silence as they undressed. Daniel's shirt drifted to the carpet and Markie's landed over it, a contrast in colour and size. The rest of their clothing fell away as easily. There was no awkwardness, no hurry, only an ineffable sense of rightness at what was happening and what was to come.

A minute and a heartbeat later, they studied each other in the moonlight. Markie's skin, normally pale ivory, became pure alabaster in its subtle glow. She looked delicate, fragile, but Daniel, better than anyone now, knew her strength.

'Shadows on the snow,' he whispered wonderingly,

one long hand lifting to brush her hair from her face. 'Markie, you're—lovely.'

She smiled because she knew he believed it to be true. Privately, she thought that he was the miracle—not softened by the moonlight, but strengthened by it. The sculpted muscles of his chest, the tautness of his stomach, the hardness of his arms and thighs were highlighted and shadowed. He was everything a man should be, everything she had wanted for so long without realising.

She caught his hand against her cheek and pressed an intimate kiss to his rough palm. 'I want you, Daniel.'

'You have me, love. You have me.'

She smiled with a knowledge as old as time, a smile that Eve had given Adam. 'Then I want more.'

Daniel accepted the invitation, answered the challenge, taking one step forward to erase the distance between them. Their bodies came together like two halves of a whole too long separated. It was hotly passionate and searingly gentle.

Markie lost herself in his eyes.

'Daniel, this feels—good.'

He smiled at the shattering understatement. 'I think so too.' With one small adjustment, he turned up the heat. 'Tell me what you want from me, Markie. I promise I'll give it all.'

Her heart was pounding. . .or was it Daniel's? They were so close that it was impossible to separate their heartbeats—and they still, she realised hungrily, had so far to go.

'I want to kiss you,' she told him with rising need, and acted on her words.

They came together like old lovers long apart, or new lovers long anticipated. Quietly, thoroughly, Markie learned the taste and texture of Daniel's mouth. She felt his warmth, and then his heat as his tongue brushed with aching gentleness against her own. She gave him her warmth in return.

Breathing roughened, bodies pressed close, fingers entwined. She moved against him once, twice in an instinctive search, and he gasped into her mouth.

'Daniel. . .I want to lie down with you.'

He eased away with difficulty to stare into her face and read the emotion there. He saw desire and hunger and certainty, a reflection of his own swirling needs. Carelessly he turned the covers down and exposed the ivory sheets.

They eased on to the mattress and lay on their sides, once again taking time to explore. Seconds, minutes, hours could have passed as they lay full length, exposed to each other.

'Your hair,' whispered Daniel, running the dark strands through his fingers like liquid silk. 'So soft.'

Markie's hand searched over his broad chest, feeling the curls there springing against her palm. 'You're hard here, Daniel,' she told him, before settling her fingers over his nipple. 'And here. I didn't realise——'

Daniel brushed her own nipple, watching with delight as it tautened and turned rosy. 'Like you, Markie.'

She drew a shaky breath, aware of a tautening in other parts of her body, a warmth, a blossoming.

'Tell me more of what you want, sweetheart,' he encouraged roughly. 'I want to know what to give you.'

Markie watched his fingers move over her breast and thought he knew exactly what she wanted and exactly how to give it to her. What he was doing to her was shattering. She wanted to shatter in return.

'I don't. . .know a lot about making love,' she murmured awkwardly. 'But with you, I——'

'Ssh! I know, Markie,' he soothed against her temple.

'I know you're not experienced. We'll take it slow, and easy. We'll make it right.'

'I want—so much, Daniel,' she told him huskily, shaken by his gentleness. 'Will you let me show you?'

He drew a steadying breath. 'We have all night, Markie. Show me.'

She took him at his word. Without fear, without shyness, she flowed over him, her slight weight cushioned by his strength. She held his eyes as her head lowered and her lips met his, and saw the passion and the need reflected in herself.

As their mouths touched, so did their bodies. With silent, searing intensity, they explored each other with every sense. Where Markie was soft, at breast and stomach and hip, Daniel was hard.

Daniel was hard. . .

Her mouth left his with tearing slowness to move to his jaw, his neck, his shoulders. At his chest, her lips swept down and captured his nipple, soothing an almost painful nibble with a tender kiss. She worked her way across his chest with tongue and teeth and lips, her silky hair brushing his jaw.

While she licked at his nipple like a curious kitten, her hands sought his ribs. She felt the shudder that shook him as if it came from within herself. With instincts she didn't question, she moved down his body with soothing kisses, arousing touches, sanity-stealing tastes that caused him to tremble beneath her.

With her cheek against his abdomen, she pressed a hot little kiss to his hipbone, and knew she had pushed him too far. She felt his long fingers entwine themselves in her hair as he pulled her slowly up his body, her breasts caressing him hip to stomach to chest. And beyond.

'Come here,' he demanded huskily, the words sliding

fiercely against her from her throat to her nipples. He tasted her as if she were the sweetest candy, small hot licks that fired flames within the heart of her body and soul. 'God, you taste so sweet!'

'Daniel. . .' It was all she could say, all she could think of as he worshipped her body.

'So pretty,' he murmured, licking her breast, then blowing on it gently to watch the nipple peak higher. He nibbled his way to her other breast and offered it similar attention. When she was throbbing and pressing hungrily against him, he captured her lips with his and whispered into her mouth, 'You want me, sweetheart. I can see how much you want me.'

'I want you,' she echoed passionately.

'Here?' he teased, allowing his tongue to dance against her own.

'Yes, there.'

'And here?' he asked, his fingers brushing the tips of her breasts, knowing that she was so sensitised with desire it would be like a brush of flames.

'Oh, yes! There.'

'Where else?' he whispered, his lips roaming again down her body.

Markie captured his hand and pressed it low on her body, where she ached, hungry for fulfilment.

'Daniel, I want you here. Can I have you here?'

His eyes flared with passion at her gaze. 'I told you I'd give you it all, love,' he promised hoarsely.

Between their bodies, his hand moved, gentle, creative fingers seeking and finding her sweet warmth. Markie's eyes dilated at the incredible sensation of Daniel's rough fingers caressing the most intimate part of her. A low, soft sigh escaped her lips as he brushed one finger over the sensitive bud and loosed the lightning.

'Daniel, I want to touch you too.' Her voice was plaintive and husky, as she trembled against his fingers.

'Then touch me,' he invited huskily. 'Anywhere, any way you want.'

'You don't mind?'

He laughed breathlessly. 'I might—survive it!'

Markie pressed a kiss to his mouth and pushed away from his body, deftly evading his outreached hands. 'So I can touch you,' she reminded him gently, settling on her knees as she straddled his body.

Daniel's eyes raced over her body, bathed in moonlight and desire. She was the most beautiful thing he had ever seen, he thought humbly. His voice not quite steady, he asked, 'Do you feel—vulnerable like that?'

Markie saw him tremble and almost smiled. Vulnerable? No, she felt strong, alive, whole. 'No. Do you?'

Daniel felt her heat and her softness and smiled. 'No. . .and yes.' Both hands lifted to frame her face. 'Markie, I know you didn't plan this when you came to these mountains. I want you to know that I'll take the responsibility for precautions.'

'Thank you,' she accepted solemnly. 'I'll take responsibility for this. . .' She touched him in the most intimate way, her hands gentle, her eyes adoring.

Daniel tried to smile, but could only manage to tremble. 'You are responsible for that, Markie. Just as I'm responsible for this.' His fingers returned to their previous caress, relearning her softness and heat.

Blindly, shaking, she lowered herself back over Daniel, rubbing against him like a soft, sinuous kitten. Once, twice, and more their bodies meshed, a white-hot friction building between them. Markie felt passion flowing moist and hot within her, softening her body, readying her for Daniel's possession.

While she softened, he hardened, an intense, painful arousal that clenched his jaw and twisted his muscles.

'More!' They whispered the word together, into each other's mouths. Daniel reached blindly for the protection he had promised while Markie rained kisses over his body.

'Now,' he groaned. 'Oh, God—now, Markie!'

She melted over him, her legs holding him tightly, driven mad by the feel of him between her thighs. 'Now, Daniel.' She tried to surge against him, all flash and instinct, but his hands tightened on her hips, holding her back.

'Slowly,' he reminded her, eyes tender. 'Softly, Markie. Passionately.'

She gasped and then moaned as she felt the first gentle touch of his hardness inside her. Just an inch, just a fraction of what she so desperately wanted from him before he withdrew, evading her instinctive contraction.

'Not yet,' he whispered, breathless. 'Oh, sweetheart, don't do that yet. We have. . .all night. Patience,' he coaxed, slipping inside again, this time pressing deeper.

Markie had no patience. She was fire and hunger and need, and Daniel was that need. She tightened and surged around him aggressively, demanding all of him, taking all of him.

He groaned and cursed. Markie gasped and shifted, shuddering with the sensations her movement evoked.

'Oh, Daniel. . .'

'Markie, are you—is it all right?' His eyes were glazed with passion, his voice muffled with tenderness.

'All right?' she repeated incredulously, shaking with hunger. 'It's—wonderful! Can't you feel me tremble?'

Daniel kissed her deeply, passionately. 'I feel you,' he answered intimately. 'Inside and out.'

He began to move, initiating a rhythm that stole her

sanity. Her world narrowed down to Daniel, beneath her, inside her. Everything but pleasure faded: the moonlight, the rustle of the sheets, the quiet of the night.

Suddenly he surged upward, rolling her beneath him. She wrapped herself around him and pulled him deeper, meeting him with fire and demand.

'Markie, it's so good!'

She clenched around him. 'Perfect,' she whispered. 'So right.'

In the heat of the darkness, in the cold fire of moonlight, Markie lost her sense of two beings coming together. On every level they touched and entwined. They were one: one body, one mind.

When the climax came it was. . .completion, sharing. Homecoming.

It took a long time to calm down. Markie still trembled in Daniel's arms and he held her close, pressing sweet, fierce kisses to her flushed skin.

'I can't believe no woman has snapped you up,' she whispered into his mouth, shaking.

He buried his face in her tumbled hair and breathed in her wild flower scent. 'The music, Markie. I've been waiting for the music.'

Through the shadows of sleep that sheltered Markie, a single note slipped in. In hesitant succession others followed, drawing her into wakefulness.

For a moment she lay still in the darkness, caught between dream and reality. Instinctively, she turned her head, eyes and body reaching out for Daniel. Sharp awareness sliced through the last vestiges of drowsiness as she found him gone.

That realisation had barely registered when she heard the music. It was the call of those hesitant notes that had awakened her, she realised now. Still and silent, she listened to the uneven melody, aware of a fragile pattern being formed.

Daniel. She sighed, missing him from her arms and her body. It was Daniel, fumbling with his piano in the darkness, drawing forth the music. She wondered now, as she had before, if the melody was being surrendered from the piano or from Daniel. She knew he believed he had coaxed the instrument into giving up the music, but she thought the opposite was true. That beautiful music was inside Daniel, waiting for release. The piano was simply the key that he used to unlock the door.

She ached a little in places that had never ached before, and it was a glorious reminder of the hours she had spent in his arms. Soundlessly, she slipped from beneath the tousled blankets and reached for his discarded shirt. She fastened the buttons absently as she left the room, drawn by the lonely notes of the piano. She mounted the stairs to the music-room quietly in the darkness, unwilling to disturb Daniel's work, unwilling to stop the beautiful, beckoning music.

In the doorway she stopped to study him across the room. The only light was cast from the fireplace. Its golden glow caressed the ivory keys of the piano and the strong fingers teasing them. He wore only jeans, and his chest caught the gleam of firelight. It also lighted his face, and she saw the frustration there as the music broke off abruptly.

His fingers crashed down on the keys and he cursed beneath his breath. Apparently the song he was writing was not going well. Markie watched as his eyes closed and his jaw tightened, and she felt the waves of emotion emanating from him.

In that moment she was tempted to go to him, to ease the frustration from him. He demanded too much of himself in order to achieve the depth of emotion he insisted on in his music.

She had, in fact, taken one unconscious step towards him, when his shoulders squared determinedly and his eyes opened. His attention focused solely on the keys beneath his fingers, he began once again to bring the song to life. The sweet, sad notes quivered at his fingertips, and drifted to Markie, weaving a gentle web around her.

Caught in his creation, she fully understood its meaning. Daniel must have understood long ago. If he pushed himself relentlessly to write his songs, if he demanded so much of himself, it was because he *was* his music, and his music was him. They were more than reflections of each other; they were one.

Knowing this, feeling this, Markie felt suddenly as if she had discovered a precious piece of Daniel. She remembered the first day they had met, when she had accused him of being a hermit. He had laughed then, and finally she understood. No hermit who ever lived shared with the world all of himself, as Daniel did with his music. He might have stopped performing, but she wondered if he understood that he still gave up pieces of himself with every note he played.

She stood in the doorway and lost track of time, absorbing the sudden knowledge of Daniel. He would fumble in the dark with his piano until this piece of himself was complete in song. But in the empty space it left behind, what would he replace it with?

The music was beautiful. Without words, Markie felt the passion, the joy, the fear, and the hunger it voiced. Daniel's passion, she thought hazily. Daniel's fear. . .

Soundlessly, she took a step back, intending to leave him with his music. But somehow, even through his hesitant melody, he became aware of her presence.

The music stopped as his head turned, and their eyes held in silence across the firelit room. Instantly the memory of their earlier lovemaking flashed between them, bridging the distance, and Markie's mouth softened as Daniel's eyes flared.

Finally, their gazes faltered and both spoke simultaneously, their words crossing.

'I didn't mean to wake you.'

'I didn't mean to disturb you.'

Daniel shrugged, taking his fingers from the keys. Markie shot him a shy smile.

'The song you were playing——'

'Trying to play,' he corrected, a lost expression in his eyes. 'It wasn't quite. . .right.'

'It was beautiful,' she told him, moving hesitantly into the room. 'It's funny, but I actually heard words in the music.'

His face went blank. 'Did you?'

She was at his side now, her fingers brushing idly over the satin-smooth wood of the piano. 'Yes.'

'What did you hear?'

She chose not to answer. Instead, she fixed her gaze on him steadily, a question in its depths. 'Is that how you write songs, Daniel? Do you find the music and then listen to the words inside it?'

He smiled. He had never heard a more accurate description of his work. 'I guess I do,' he conceded. 'I've never really analysed the process before.'

'The words come from the music, and the music comes from you,' she mused softly.

He shifted restlessly, on uncertain ground. 'The piano——'

Markie cut him off with just a look. 'Is an instrument. It doesn't think or feel or create. Not like the man who uses it.'

'I feel. . .' he whispered almost silently, reaching for her hand. 'Why aren't we in bed?'

She smiled. 'Because your piano called to you. Maybe you needed it more than you needed sleep.'

'I didn't want you to wake up alone.'

'I'm used to it,' she dismissed lightly, squeezing his hand.

'And that's why I didn't want you to do it,' he told her, pulling her gently on to the bench. 'I wanted you to wake up in my arms.'

Markie's head dropped to his shoulder, and she sighed as she felt his arms tighten around her. 'It's not morning yet.'

Daniel turned her face up to his and kissed her gently, his mouth treasuring hers. 'Let's not waste the night, Markie.'

She felt the emotion, saw the fire, touched the hunger stirring inside him. Lithely she rose and clasped his large hands in hers, drawing him to his feet. 'Come with me.'

Daniel didn't move forward, but his hands tightened to draw her closer. 'Stay with me,' he whispered into her mouth, holding her tight.

Markie was almost lost. The passion was building between them, catching fire from the ember left glowing. Vaguely, as Daniel's lips explored her face, she thought the ember would always be there, waiting to explode into flame. And all it would take, as long as she lived, would be the touch of Daniel's hand.

'Kiss me, Markie,' he whispered against her mouth. 'Love me.'

She trembled against him with the onslaught of memories and anticipation. Her fingers twined with his and tightened with one last effort at control. 'Daniel, come to bed.'

He shuddered at the words, his eyes closed. 'I don't

know if I can make it that far, Markie. Make love with me here.'

'In——' She broke off with a sigh as he nibbled at her bottom lip, then eased the sweet hurt with his tongue. 'In front of the piano? Daniel, we can't! It's very impressionable, you know.'

His eyes opened languidly. 'What about you, Markie?' He drew her hips into intimate contact with his own and moved with a drugging rhythm. 'Am I making any impression on you, darling?'

Oh, yes, he was making an impression on her. Through the fine material of his borrowed shirt, she felt every inch of muscle and bone pressed against her. Hungrily, she matched his rhythm with one of her own. Her hands moved to the waist of his jeans, slowly moving down the five-button fly. 'Daniel. . .'

He muffled the sound of his name with his mouth, taking hers with softness and strength. 'What about the piano?' he asked, shivering as her hands caressed him.

'Damn the piano,' she muttered, trembling beneath his hands and lips. 'I want you, Daniel.'

Slowly, deliberately, he unfastened the buttons down the front of her shirt and edged the material away from her flushed skin. As the material landed in a pool behind her, he smiled into her eyes.

'I meant, what about the piano as opposed to the floor?' he explained softly, turning her to measure the gleaming wood surface.

Markie met his gaze with hunger and shock and pleasure in her face. 'Daniel. . .I like the way you think.'

And she pressed against him.

CHAPTER NINE

FOR Markie, everything changed after that night. It was as if a veil had been lifted from her heart and mind. She experienced a crystal clarity of sight and taste and touch, a pure intensity of thought and emotion.

In truth, it was simply that she began to live in the present instead of the future. Happiness wasn't some day, but now, in Daniel's eyes, in his smile, in his arms. And more, much more happiness was within herself.

Somewhere deep in the back of her mind, she knew that this time would end, that her search would once again beckon. But for now, for this precious moment out of time, there were no regrets. The decision had been made and they were lovers in the best sense of the word.

Sometimes Markie would wake up, reaching for Daniel, only to be met with empty space. She knew he had gone to his piano, and she waited. When he came back to her—and he always did—she pretended to be asleep. She remembered how important it was to him that she should not wake up alone. Knowing this, she thought that whatever drove him from their bed must be powerful indeed.

Every night, Daniel awoke in the early morning hours to find her asleep, clinging to the side of the mattress with the distance of the bed between them. And every night, he gently brought her back into his arms, silently offering things he couldn't give voice to. Some day, he determined in the darkness of the room, Markie would rest against him and know that she was home.

The murderer was quietly stalking his prey. With soundless steps he moved ever closer to her until he was inches from her back. Gloved fingers reached to cover her mouth. . .

A hand fell on Markie's shoulder and she jumped in terror. Instinctively she whirled, crouching low and firm in her fighting stance. Her front foot slashed out in a dazzling sidekick to the abdomen of her accoster, the heel perfectly positioned for greatest impact.

Several events occurred simultaneously. Markie's eyes lighted on Daniel's surprised face as her foot lashed forward. Her heel landed squarely on his unprotected torso despite her last-second attempt to break off the attack. And he crumpled to the ground, doubled neatly in two.

'Oh, my God! Daniel, are you OK?' Markie was on her knees in an instant, her hands covering his at his stomach.

Daniel was too winded to form words. He could only look at her with reproachful eyes and gasp for breath.

'Oh, I'm so sorry!' she cried, trying to pry his hands away so that she could massage the abused area. 'You sneaked up behind me and I was writing a frightening scene in the book and I wasn't thinking, and it was instinctive to kick out like that—and don't you know that you shouldn't *do* things like that to a person with an imagination as active as mine?'

Somewhere in the middle of her endless explanation, Daniel regained the ability to speak. As it was, he had to wait until Markie ran out of breath before he had the opportunity.

His stomach ached and her nearness was disturbing, the touch of her hands on his flesh was almost as stunning as the kick itself, yet the only words he could force were, 'You really do have a blue belt in Tae Kwondo.'

She looked ridiculously shamefaced. 'I'm afraid so. Daniel, does it hurt?'

Less and less, he answered silently, but meeting her concerned gaze he only mustered a pathetic nod.

She looked more distressed. She read what she perceived as stoic bravery in his eyes, and melted. Her fingers pushed the dark hair from his forehead and she placed a tender kiss to his temple, treating him for all the world like a toddler who had taken a spill.

Daniel managed to suffer it all with the same stoicism—and contrived to pull an even more pathetic expression to his face. 'I'm OK,' he offered bravely, burying his face against her shoulder to hide his expression of pleasure from her examining gaze.

'It still hurts, doesn't it?'

In fact, Markie had managed to pull her punch somewhat and the pain was gone. Daniel only sighed.

She bit her lip. 'Come on, Daniel, let's get you off of the floor.' She grasped his hand and pulled his arm around her shoulder, providing a crutch as he lumbered to his feet. As gently as possible, she manoeuvred him into the living-room and on to the couch. Once she had ruthlessly fluffed the cushions beneath his head, she stood over him, wringing her hands.

'Oh, what can I do? Would you like some fruit juice or an aspirin? Maybe a heating pad or. . .'

Before matters got out of hand, Daniel decided he should make a suggestion of his own. 'I don't think any of that would help,' he sighed wearily. 'Maybe you could. . .no, forget it.'

'What?' she rushed. 'What do you think would help?'

He risked her a glance. 'Well. . .maybe you could kiss it better.' Total silence greeted the suggestion. He met her eyes innocently. 'It's the least you can do.'

Markie murmured soothingly and dropped to his side, relieved that he was up to such shenanigans. 'I always try to do the least I can do,' she assured him virtuously. Her hands drifted lightly to his chest as her mouth lowered to tease his. 'I just can't seem to remember exactly where I kicked you.'

'I guess we'll just have to explore until we figure it out,' he offered bravely.

'You're so intrepid,' she remarked admiringly, nuzzling his jaw.

'I. . .know.'

'Maybe we should start here,' she suggested, brushing her lips against his and catching the sigh that left them.

'I don't think that's it,' he managed, drowning in her taste.

'Does it still hurt?'

Daniel smothered a groan. 'Now it—aches.'

'Well, we'll keep trying,' Markie promised, her lips sliding against the hard line of his jaw.

It took quite a while to reach the point of impact. Markie forgot to stop her ministrations when she got there, and Daniel didn't remind her.

They lived in passionate harmony for days. And then something unexpected happened, and the happiness they had built was shattered in the space of one lost and revealing afternoon.

Markie spied the flash of movement in the trees from the corner of her eye and came to an abrupt halt. Yes, there it was again! She focused intently on the scrap of honey-brown fur visible through the thick woods. Smaller than a deer, she thought curiously, and too delicate to be a bighorn. Cautiously, she inched forward. . .

Daniel's fingers crashed on to the keys abruptly, emitting a discordant sound. Curiously he tilted his head. Had Markie called to him from downstairs? In silence, he listened. And in listening, heard nothing but silence.

He rose from the bench and crossed to the stairs. The song was going well—was almost finished, in fact—but he'd rather spend time with Markie any day.

Eagerly, he started down the stairs.

Markie watched as the animal bolted awkwardly away, putting some distance between them. It was a fawn, she noted in concern, and apparently alone in the forest. And there was something very wrong with the way it moved, the awkward gait it employed to separate itself from her. As the animal moved again, restlessly shifting its stance, she realilsed what was wrong.

He was only using three legs, she thought in distress. His left foreleg was held carefully off the ground, in reaction to some unknown pain. Markie's tender heart was immediately touched. She thought of Bambi and Thumper and Flower. The fawn was so delicate and so young. Separated from his mother as he was, he must be frightened.

There was only Markie to help him, and as she watched, she thought fancifully that the fawn was asking for that help. For every step forward that she took, the fawn took one back, but he was only maintaining the distance, not increasing it. Markie understood that he was simply being cautious, that he needed time to trust in her good intentions.

If he would only let her, she thought hopefully, then she would help him. Softly, she began to tell the fawn.

* * *

The living area was empty. Daniel was not particularly surprised, since it seemed Markie preferred the music-room. When she was trying to give him the solitude she insisted he needed to write his songs, she usually retreated to the dining-room.

But the dining-room was empty as well. A sudden, unexplained worry gnawed at him.

'Markie?'

Not waiting for an answer, he stopped to look in Markie's bedroom and his own. Although they spent each night, all night together in his bed, Markie had resisted his attempts to move her clothing to his room. There was still a core of privacy within her, shaped by years of independence and solitude, that she wouldn't— or couldn't—surrender. And because he needed every-thing, Daniel worried.

When he found both rooms empty, he moved on to the kitchen. Her papers were scrambled over the table. There was a cup sitting in the sink and some bread-crumbs on the counter.

But there was no Markie.

Daniel opened the utility-room door knowing what he would find. Her jacket was gone, and her boots. She had taken his day pack as well.

Ordinarily, he wouldn't be concerned; Markie fre-quently went exploring, now that most of the snow was gone. But she almost always went with him, Daniel reminded himself. She was a free woman, an indepen-dent soul. And still unfamiliar with his land, a small voice returned.

What worried him was the instinct that had inter-rupted his work, drawing him to find her. It wasn't something he could explain or name, just a sense of something not quite right, not quite. . .safe.

With great economy of motion, he picked up his

boots. Markie would probably flay him with her tongue, and lecture him about self-reliance, but she was about to get some company.

For twenty minutes or more Markie patiently edged closer to the fawn, only to be foiled time and again as he backed away. She didn't even notice that she was being drawn deeper into the forest, out of sight of the meadow where she had left her pack. She only wanted to help this delicate, abandoned creature whose eyes seemed to lure her on.

Suddenly, without warning, the fawn's head jerked up, his ears cocked. It was the only thing that alerted Markie to the presence of the buck and doe sheltered by the trees. She froze in instant stillness as the buck's eyes held hers across the distance. He seemed to be measuring her, assessing the threat she presented. Studying his antlers, she was quite sure she didn't want to present any threat. To convince the buck of this, she remained motionless. As the buck squared himself defensively and held his position, the doe picked her way delicately towards the fawn, who nudged her affectionately. Because Markie was a writer, and therefore given to flights of imagination, she could almost hear the reproof the doe directed at the fawn as she herded him away.

When mother and son had disappeared into the foliage, the buck seemed to blink and casually dip his head in salute. Markie watched in astonishment as he ambled off after his family.

Then she smiled. The fawn would be well cared for, she decided in relief. Whatever was wrong with that leg would be attended to naturally, as it was meant to be. He hadn't needed Markie so much as she had needed to believe in her own ability and willingness to help.

Considering this bit of insight, she turned to retrace her steps back to the meadow.

And realised that she was lost.

He had known she would come to the meadow. It hadn't taken much in the way of tracking skills to follow her there. The progress of the wild flowers held such importance for her and, in truth, for him as well.

Daniel caught sight of his day pack on the ground, abandoned. He looked around thoroughly, but there was no other sign of her presence.

'Markie!' The call carried on the still mountain air, but elicited no response.

He studied the sky in rising concern. It was clear enough, but darkness was already beginning to creep around the edges of the day. Within an hour, dusk would settle. Markie, he knew, was not a practical woman. Warm, vibrant, imaginative, comforting, exciting, brash, intelligent, kind—but not practical. She was probably off searching for wild flowers, without thought of the setting sun.

And he wouldn't want her any other way, he admitted to himself. The expression on his face, the gentleness in his eyes would have frightened Markie had she been there to see it.

But Markie was wandering frustratedly through the woods, trying to find her way back to the meadow.

'I should have left a trail of breadcrumbs,' she mumbled to herself. 'So what if I left my peanut butter and jelly sandwich in my pack at the meadow? I should have bent branches or marked Xs on tree-trunks with a rock or watched more Tarzan movies as a child or——' She broke off, out of tenderfoot ideas. Besides, she reminded herself, 'should have' was a phrase she assiduously avoided. It profited no one and changed nothing.

She was lost. And she would find her way out. She was an intelligent woman who had travelled over most of the country. She was good under pressure, and she was possessed of a keen mind, sharp instincts, and——

'No sense of direction,' she finished with a moan.

This would never happen to Daniel, she thought despairingly. Because this was his land, his home, and he knew every inch of it.

She wondered, quite suddenly, what it would be like to know every inch of Daniel. They were lovers now, as well as friends, and he was generous in loving. She knew the breadth of his shoulders and the hard ridge of his ribcage; the shape of his hair-roughened calf and the calluses on his fingers from the piano and the snow shovel. His body held no mystery for her, and he had opened a great deal of his mind as well. But Markie was aware of a part of Daniel that he held back, something he chose not to share in bed or out. And because she needed everything, she worried.

If only. She bit off a sigh—another useless phrase. When she got back to the house, maybe she would ask Daniel about that part he never shared. Or maybe she would just lie in his arms and pray that he never asked for what she couldn't share. When she got back to the house. . .

It was getting dark. Daniel would begin to worry soon, she thought regretfully. But he knew his land, and in an odd sort of way, he knew Markie. If only——she broke off that thought and eyed a nearby tree suspiciously. Hadn't she seen that pine before? She was quite sure. . .wasn't she?

* * *

There were still patches of snow on the ground, Daniel noted thankfully. Not a lot, but enough to enable him to track Markie's progress through the trees. Why she had gone into the forest at all was the mystery. If it really had been to search for wild flowers, they were going to have a serious discussion when he found her. A discussion all about wild animals and broken ankles and falling darkness and worried friends and lovers.

Friend and lover. Until Markie he hadn't known a single person could be both.

Shaking that enticing thought away, Daniel studied the ground. It was soft from melting snow, and the prints quite clear. Deer, he decided, and Markie. Looking more closely, he realised that Markie's prints crossed over one another, heading in different directions. Following the trail that seemed freshest, he soon ran across other conflicting markings, footprints heading first north, then south, then east. The strides were even, the gait steady. She wasn't hurt, he thought in relief, just lost. For Markie, he thought that would probably be worse.

Fifteen minutes from total darkness, Markie was muttering to herself again. She was certain of two facts: moss grew on the north side of a tree, and Daniel's house was west of the meadow.

'Now,' she told herself bracingly, 'putting those two facts together, we can determine that I should. . .oh, damn! I don't know what we can determine.'

She was sure of one other thing. If she waited long enough, Daniel would come for her. It was only a matter of time before he realised that she was not in the house. Trying to judge the hour by the depth of the darkness, she decided that he would be slipping into the kitchen right about now, ready to begin the evening meal. When he didn't find her there, he would check the rest of the house and find her jacket gone. Worried about the darkness, he would come for her. He would find her.

Quietly exhausted, Markie leaned against a nearby pine. If she waited, Daniel would find her. . .and not find her.

Fourteen minutes later, Daniel caught a flash of red through the trees and picked up his pace. It was Markie. He knew even before he was close enough to make out her features. She was leaning against a pine, standing, not sitting, as if determined not to give in to that point. Stubborn, lovely Markie.

He stopped scant inches in front of her and met her eyes. Her face was solemn, almost expressionless as she studied him. The very lack of emotion she exhibited alarmed him more than anything else.

'Markie, are you OK?'

Markie heard the sudden concern in his tone, saw it on his face, but couldn't find the words to reassure him, or herself. 'I'm lost.'

With the sun beyond the horizon, the night was cold. Daniel drew one finger down her flushed cheek and smiled gently. 'Not any more, Markie. I've got you.'

She was silent for a long time. 'Yes,' she agreed at length, her voice weary in a way he didn't understand. 'I knew you'd find me.'

'Come on,' he hustled her to her right. 'Let's get back to the meadow.'

'Is it far?' she asked with a marked lack of interest.

He shot her a quick glance. 'No, not far. You were headed in the right direction.'

Markie smiled thinly. 'I wonder.'

Daniel had no trouble sensing her pensive mood, but couldn't restrain his anger at her foolishness. 'Markie, what took you so far into the forest? Why did you go wandering through unfamiliar ground without your pack, and so close to nightfall?'

They had advanced several yards before she answered. 'I guess I just wasn't thinking. My—instincts have been off lately.' She touched his arm tentatively. 'I'm sorry to be such a bother, Daniel.'

He jerked her to a stop and pressed a hard little kiss to her lips. 'You're not a bother, Markie. You're a wonder.' He kissed her again, then pushed her forward. 'Move, wild flower. It's getting cold out here.'

By the time they picked up Markie's pack from the meadow and found their way back to the house, Daniel thought she had shaken herself free of the odd mood that made her so distant.

She had not.

In the days that followed, Markie replayed that afternoon over and over again in her mind. She didn't fault her decision to follow the fawn into the woods, or even her inability to find her way out again. Such was the tenor of Markie's life. She accepted her occasional impulsiveness and the responsibilities that it carried. At times, she revelled in that side of her nature, because it made life interesting and unpredictable.

But she always came back to those final minutes, when she had abdicated that responsibility to Daniel's hands, and waited for him to find her.

The last few weeks had given her much, but Markie was now painfully aware of what they had taken. Whether or not Daniel asked for it, whether or not she wanted it, she had given over too much of herself. She found, after all, that her sense of responsibility and independence rested not in her hands, but in her heart. And her heart rested with Daniel.

For another woman, it might have been an even trade. For Markie, with the ghosts of dependence and determination haunting her, it was a betrayal.

She wasn't simply losing the battles of the past, but the hope for the future. She was sacrificing, not only her independence, but her search as well. She could feel herself slipping into Daniel's life, Daniel's home, Daniel's priorities, and in doing so losing touch with her own.

The thought of living without him was agonising. But the alternative, she feared, would destroy all that she had fought to achieve over her lifetime. She had demanded the price of love and found herself too poor to pay it.

And since she didn't believe in falling back, the only road left to her was a painful advance. . .past love, past Daniel.

Two days passed. Two nights. Until one early dawn, when Daniel woke up alone. His heart pounding painfully inside his chest, he searched for his missing lover.

He found her, as he had known he would, at the piano. She hadn't bothered to turn on a light or build a fire, so the room was shadowed with cold dawn. Her fingers moved over the keys, but not with the intention of drawing forth music. She wasn't playing the piano so much as caressing it.

Daniel wondered fancifully if she could feel the echoes of warmth from his fingers, if she could hear the ghosts of emotions he had poured out on those keys.

Markie, he wondered in silent despair, why won't you let me bridge this distance between us?

He made no sound, no move, but Markie went very still, then dropped her hands.

'Daniel.' She spoke his name with a softness that drew him forward.

'I missed you,' he told her, standing close enough to touch her, yet holding himself back.

'I think it's time for me to go, Daniel.' Her voice was carefully controlled, but her body was taut.

'Go?' he repeated blankly, as stunned by the words as he would have been by a jackhammer to the heart. 'Why?'

'It's time,' she repeated simply.

His eyes narrowed. 'This has something to do with your getting lost in the forest, doesn't it? You've been— different since then.'

Markie studied her hands as they clenched upon one another. 'That's part of it.'

'I don't understand!' Daniel exclaimed, his hands curling around her shoulders and forcing her to face him. 'What does that have to do with your leaving?'

'It doesn't——'

'Dammit, Markie!' he roared, shaking her gently to draw her eyes. 'Tell me!'

'All right,' she conceded, a little flame licking to life behind her eyes. 'I got myself lost in that forest, Daniel. But I didn't find my way out. I had to be rescued.'

His face was blank with incomprehension. 'That happens to the best of us sometimes.'

'Not to me!' she told him in passionate denial. 'It's never happened to me before. All my life, I've accepted responsibility for my own actions. If I got into something, it was up to me to get out of it.'

'Markie!'

She continued without acknowledging his interruption. 'In the forest, I didn't even try to get out by myself.'

'That's not true,' Daniel denied. 'I followed your

tracks, remember? You searched a long time for the meadow, and you were on the right track when I found you.'

'When you found me,' she repeated with great clarity. 'When you found me I was leaning against a tree, waiting for you. Because I knew you would come. I knew you would take me out of there.'

'And I did,' he pointed out in frustration. 'What's wrong with that?'

'Don't you see? I should have found my own way. I shouldn't have given up. I relied on you instead of relying on myself,' she admitted painfully. 'And that's wrong.'

'Is it?' he challenged. 'Why? I rely on you for things.'

She stilled. 'What things?'

'Friendship. Warmth. Understanding. Peace of mind.' His eyes were quizzical. 'Is that wrong, Markie?'

Markie swallowed an edge of despair. 'It's not the same thing. Don't you see?' she asked achingly. 'You quit touring because it took pieces of you away. Well, I'm giving up pieces of myself to you. First it was friendship, then passion. Daniel, I can't give up my independence. Not even to you. Especially not to you. If I give you that, asked for or not, what comes next? How much of myself will I lose?'

His hands tightened almost painfully around her delicate bones, then abruptly loosened their grip. He whirled and paced across the room. 'Lose? Is that what you think? That I want to *take* from you?'

Markie crossed her arms over her chest to ward off the chill Daniel's distance brought. God, she hurt inside. Empty, she felt so empty watching his back, measuring the distance between them. But she was right to do this. She had to be. If she had given up any more of herself, given up all that had screamed for surrender, she doubted that she would be able to survive the resulting emptiness.

Daniel listened to the silence and felt a wave of despair. 'You know what I think?'

'Hardly ever,' she admitted sadly.

'I think we've talked too much about losing and not enough about gaining.' His mouth tightened. 'My fault, I guess. It took me a long time to understand. . .'

'Understand what?'

He squared his shoulders. 'Markie, you're afraid I'm taking things from you. Well, maybe I am. A little of your independence, a little of the distance you surround yourself with. But, dammit, I'm giving too! You said so yourself. You're happier, you're not lonely any more. Isn't that worth a fraction of your independence? God, you think that independence is a strength, and it is, up to a point. But you use it like a weapon against yourself. And all it wins for you is loneliness. Isn't that what hurts you the most: not letting me in, but locking me out?'

Markie stared at him, stunned. It was true, she thought. Everything he said was true. It was her sense of independence that was forcing her away from him, forcing her back into loneliness. And Daniel had offered her something of himself for every piece she gave up, but she had been too blind to see it. Unable to believe that he could. . .complete her.

As he misread her continued silence, Daniel's face darkened with frustration. 'You know, I feel like I'm losing shards of my independence and solitude to you. And that's painful for me, because I remember too well what it was like before, when I was touring. I remember how empty it left me.'

'But you're not running away.' There was a dawning comprehension in Markie's voice now, a little flicker of light in her eyes that Daniel, in his desperation, didn't see.

'No, I'm not running away. Because it's not the same thing. Those places offered me nothing. They took and left me empty.' His mouth softened. 'I give to you, Markie. And you give to me. We replace solitude with intimacy, independence with strength. I don't see anything to run from. Do you?'

She didn't, not when she finally understood. Within her grasp was the long-held goal. . .completion. But what about her desperate need for belonging and home? A slash of pain slammed through her. Would it come down to trading off need against need? Could she ever really be complete without finding her home?

Voice shaking, she asked, 'What about my search? How can I let go of that and still be whole, Daniel? I would be trading one part of myself for another. In the end, I wouldn't have gained anything.'

'You think I'm trying to make you give up your search, don't you, wild flower?'

She flinched from the endearment and fought for control. 'I think staying any longer would mean giving it up,' she answered at last. 'And I can't do that. I've searched for so long. . .'

Daniel nodded, his head moving fractionally. 'Searched. Yes, you've searched. With your eyes and your heart and your mind closed.' He turned back and crossed to her, pulling her into his arms. With his lips against her silky hair, he whispered, 'Markie, isn't it time to stop searching and start finding?'

'I'm trying to do that.'

'Then why haven't you?' he challenged. 'How many places have you found and deserted in the past six years? How many people have you touched and left?'

'You make it sound like——'

'Your childhood?' he suggested. 'Isn't it like that, Markie? Moving from place to place, person to person, before you risk belonging anywhere, with anyone?'

'Risk?' she echoed disbelievingly. 'You don't know what you're talking about.'

'Don't I? I'm talking about the risk that holding on presents to someone who's perfected the art of letting go. First your mother: you let go of her when you were three years old. Then Griff, when you were seven. Then every foster home where you were ever placed. Markie,' he murmured achingly, 'I understand why you let go of those places. The only other choice was to be torn away. You were a child and your life was in someone else's hands. But what about now? Why are you letting go now?'

'What do I have to hold on to here?' she burst out.

'Me.'

'Your home, your life, your priorities. What about mine?'

'Are you really that blind?' he asked despairingly. 'Don't you see what we have here?'

Markie's eyes shadowed regretfully. She was hurting him, and hurting herself. 'Daniel, what we have together is wonderful. I didn't know I could feel such——' She broke off, struggling against the word that fought to emerge. 'But it's not everything. You hold back part of yourself and I hold back part of me. I can't give any more because I don't have any more. I'm missing something vital, something that could make me whole.'

'And that is?'

'Home. Belonging. Things you can't give me, Daniel.'

He was silent for so long that she thought he had given up. Thinking this, she felt an odd ache around her heart. 'I'll pack.' She had taken one stumbling step when he spoke.

'Wait!'

Markie stopped reluctantly, poised on the edge of despair and torn ragged by conflicting needs.

'There's something I want to give you. Something—I need to tell you.'

CHAPTER TEN

MARKIE watched with wary eyes as Daniel crossed the room to stand before the cabinets that lined one wall. There, he pushed back two shuttered doors to reveal an impressive array of electronic equipment. One component was a sophisticated reel-to-reel tape recorder, more complicated than any Markie had ever seen.

'I don't like to write the score of a song as I'm working on it,' he told her abruptly, gesturing to the recorder. 'So I record it here and score it later.'

Markie watched him, bewildered.

Daniel studied her, a stricken expression on his face, as if he was regretting the entire situation. 'The thing I wanted to give you is here, on the tape.' He searched her eyes quietly, looking for something she didn't understand.

'A song?'

'A suite of songs,' he corrected, shifting uneasily. 'They flow into one another, build from the first to the last to tell a story.'

'You're giving them to me?' she asked uncertainly.

'I wrote them for you. Well, that's not quite true,' he recanted raggedly. 'In the beginning, I was writing for myself. I was. . .confused and I needed to understand. When I did, I began to write for you, because I wanted you to understand as well.'

'Are these the songs for your next album?'

'No!' he denied roughly. 'I told you, they're yours. I'll never record them, never tour the country and spill this part of us out to anyone who has the price of a ticket.

I've given up enough of myself to strangers. I won't sacrifice you as well. But this is a conversation I needed to have with you.' He sighed almost soundlessly. 'I wrote the first song before we met, and the second that first night of the storm. After that. . .well, I guess you'll be able to determine the sequence.'

He drew a shallow breath and reached for the play button. In the waiting silence that followed that first click, he studied her face, as though he was memorising every feature, every expression.

When he turned away to stare blindly out of the window, Markie watched helplessly. Her eyes focused on his back with a need and hunger she for once didn't fight to hide.

The first note broke between them, as soft and as poignant as a child's cry. It hinted at an emptiness, a lack of strength, the sense of something vital missing. And then Daniel's voice joined the music, filling the room and filling Markie's heart. The song was called 'Half a Heart'.

With life's first breath a man is blessed
Whole heart and shiny soul,
But the price of life is sacrifice
Of the fragile whole.
And so are pieces lost and spent
To defray a bitter toll.

Through rite of passage and through doubt
We play a lying game,
Yielding fragments here and there
In hopes of dodging pain,
And deceive ourselves 'cause pieces lost
Are never found again.

There are shards of me littering
Rooms and halls and alleys.
It's those forgotten places that
Drive me to my knees.
And steal a part, 'bout half a heart
From what I used to be.

Half a heart that tries to hide
The emptiness that reigns inside,
A tattered soul and hollow space
Tainted, lost and then displaced,
A broken man who's crying tears
For all the spent and shattered years.

But at day's end we understand
The bargain that we've wrought
In selling fractions of our lives
We negate the balance that we sought,
And in the light that comes from truth
We find we've been reduced to half a heart.

Half a heart that tries to hide
The emptiness that reigns inside,
A tattered soul and hollow space
Tainted, lost and then displaced,
A broken man who's crying tears
For all the spent and shattered years.

In the end there's no turning back,
No footprints to retrace.
We learn instead to live without
The things we can't replace,
And wonder how we came to this
As we look into hell's face.

From half a heart away. . .

Markie trembled with the last note as it faded into silence, stunned by the emotional impact of the song. Daniel rested his forehead against the cool glass of the windowpane, his body still.

She knew that Daniel had written about himself, a man who had given up pieces of himself too easily and only too late realised that he had fractured his soul in doing so. How difficult it must have been for him to write those words and offer them to Markie, exposing himself, giving up still more of what he now so jealously guarded.

She was shaking with the implications of that gift when the second song began. The song, she remembered solemnly, that Daniel had written that first night of the storm. A song, she realised with uneasy perception, about her, about that first meeting when he had tried so hard to walk away. A song called 'Hide and Seek'.

> Emerald eyes, I know you're wondering,
> But I'm not a man to take a chance
> On a woman who can see so much of me,
> So cautiously we take this frozen stance
> And curiously we measure and we stare,
> Filled with equal parts of need and fear.
>
> Emerald eyes are drawing me
> Into their wary depths,
> Calling for a chance to ease
> The loneliness that's kept
> Like a secret pain inside
> Those shattered, shuttered eyes.
>
> And emerald eyes are hiding,
> Daring me to breach
> The walls of strength and silence
> No touch could ever reach,
> And within that dark disguise
> I feel those needy, haunting eyes.

I can't let you come no closer,
I'm going to turn away.
It hurts not knowing what the rules are
To this painful game we play,
And losing all the time just leaves me weak.
Guess I just don't have the heart for hide and seek.

Emerald eyes, you scare me
'Cause I know you see too deep,
Looking past the face I show
To the man I used to be.
I think I'll just retire from the field,
A soldier, even beaten, never drops his shield.

And I can't let you come no closer,
I'm going to turn away.
It hurts not knowing what the rules are
To this painful game we play,
And losing all the time just leaves me weak.
Guess I just don't have the heart for hide and seek,
I don't have the heart for hide and seek. . .

A frightened man, Markie thought painfully. And a frightened woman. Drawing close and then away, flirting with need but heeding fear. His emotions at that first meeting had exactly matched her own, she realised. Had the snowstorm not intervened, both could have gone on hiding indefinitely. Both would have missed the intimacy they had found. Both would have been safe. . .and sorry.

The songs continued, cataloguing the journey of a man from loneliness to love. The third song talked about a man's reluctant awareness of a woman, the unthinking touches and casual smiles that made him want things he had never known.

The next was about shadows: shadows of the past, shadows of fear, shadows in a woman's eyes. A man who wanted to drive the shadows away, to bring light to darkness, to erase the past and offer a future.

The songs went on. A woman who knew too well how to let go and knew nothing of holding on. A night of love. A plea to give love a chance. A promise to build a home. Defeat as distances intruded between lovers. Fear, as the lesson of letting go claimed another victim.

A man's—Daniel's—life as he learned love and fear, hope and need, passion and defeat lay spread before her. As the last note faded away, the silence left behind tightened and deafened. Neither moved. Daniel's body remained tense, his eyes focused sightlessly through the glass. Markie, in turn, held her breath as the words and music swirled through her mind.

Daniel had given voice to every need she fought so hard to master, every emotion she struggled to hide. In doing so, he had dissolved her control, exposed her to his eyes, and her own. She felt as if she were looking into a very bright mirror and seeing herself for the first time in its harsh reflection.

Six years of her life had been spent, as Daniel had told her, searching for something with eyes, mind, and heart closed. And a closed heart, she realised painfully, was the cruellest thing of all. She had known that as a child, shuffled from place to place, unloved, lonely. When had she forgotten? What had she lost because of that blindness?

All this time, she thought achingly, Daniel had been offering her the one thing she needed above all else. Completion, yes, as she had finally understood. But he wasn't forcing her to choose between that and a home. He was giving both. He had opened himself, opened her, but she had been too stubborn to see it.

It was into that realisation that Daniel spoke, his voice

tight. He didn't turn to face her, instead offering the words to the faint reflection he found in the glass.

'I'll sign the house over to you—the land. It will be your home, Markie.' His mouth twisted bitterly. 'Fences and boundaries. Stone and wood and glass.'

Tears blurred her eyes. He was offering everything he thought she wanted. Everything she herself had thought she wanted. . .until she heard his songs. Now, with the insight he had given her, she finally understood what he had been trying to tell her all along. She had been looking for home in the wrong places, looking for a place when she should have been looking for. . .

'I won't take your home, Daniel.'

He smiled mirthlessly. 'Don't you understand yet, Markie? My home has no boundaries, no fences.' At last he came to her, reaching out to brush his fingers against her breast. 'My home is here. Can't you feel me inside you?'

She shivered with a wave of pure emotion. Yes, oh, yes, she felt Daniel inside. She would forever carry the love and the passion she felt for him. Carry the warmth and the joy and the friendship he brought her. Carry the pieces of him and herself he had given.

With his words and his music and his tenderness, Daniel had healed so many of the old hurts that she carried with her. There was only one final barrier to breach. And it was the scar that had kept her running since she was old enough to understand its pain.

She met his gaze, still and scared and aching. 'Daniel, I'm frightened.'

He ran a tender hand over her hair, soothing, arousing. 'I love you, Markie.'

The words, just to hear the words made her tremble with longing. 'I think that's why I'm afraid.'

'Why?'

Because she had listened to his songs, Markie knew that Daniel could answer that question as well as, or better than, she could herself. But she also knew that the words must come from her if there was to be any resolution at all.

'You know how I grew up. One of the first things you learn in the foster-care system is not to get attached. You always have to be ready to. . .let go.' Her face shadowed. 'Daniel, I know so little about being loved. I like to think that, in her way, my mother loved me. And I know that Griff loved me.'

'And they both let go.' His voice was dark with understanding and reflected pain.

Markie nodded, just once.

A flaring intensity fired his eyes and his voice. 'Markie, I love you. And I'm never going to let go of that, or you.' He cupped her face with both hands, forcing her to meet his eyes. 'I want to marry you. I want to be beside you always, a heartbeat and a touch away whenever you need me. *Always*, Markie.'

Her heart twisted and every bit of love she had been so desperately concealing rushed through. 'Daniel, I love you too.'

He trembled and pressed a soft kiss against her brow, smiling tenderly. 'I know.'

'You know?' she echoed. 'How could you? I've been so frightened of what I feel, I'd almost succeeded in hiding it from myself.'

'But *I* wasn't blinded by fear, Markie. I see you clearly.' His eyes were thoughtful. 'Sometimes I think I know you better than you know yourself. And the woman I know, the woman I love would never have come to me that night without love. Would she?'

Markie knew that he was referring to the night they had first made love, and, after a grave and thoughtful moment, she shook her head. 'No, she wouldn't. Not without love.'

'That's what gave me hope, Markie. And strength enough to be patient.' Concern shadowed his face. 'I knew I was in your heart, but I didn't know if you'd let me into your mind. I didn't know if you would come to understand that——'

'That I was looking for home in all the wrong places,' she finished for him, desperate to erase the shadows from his eyes. 'That the sense of belonging I need won't be found in a pile of bricks and wood, or on a scrap of dirt with those deeds and boundaries.' Her gaze searched his face, bright with love and understanding. Softly she rested her hand over his heart and felt the steady beat that matched her own. 'I understand that, Daniel. I understand that my home is here.'

He trembled beneath her touch. 'Will you marry me? Be my wife and friend and lover?'

She closed her eyes on a wave of yearning and wariness. Between them now there must be truth. 'I love you, Daniel. And I'll try my best. But I've been by myself for such a long time. There's still so much of me that needs to be independent and strong. I don't know if I can change——'

'Have I asked you to?' He shook her gently. 'Markie, I fell in love with a strong, independent woman. Why would I want to make her over into something else? I don't want to take over your life. I just want to be part of it.'

It wasn't easy for Markie to accept those words. All her life, it seemed, people had been trying to change her. But in Daniel she saw conviction and honesty and love. Swallowing past a suddenly tight throat, she whispered, 'You are. You will be. Always, Daniel.'

Daniel took her mouth with his. She felt the tremble

that shuddered through his body as he drew her near, and nearer still. It was as if he couldn't get close enough, couldn't hold tight enough, couldn't kiss deep enough. Like the waves that follow a hurricane to shore, he swept over her, possessing, overwhelming. Markie gave herself up to the storm, and revelled in its fierceness.

It was a long time before coherent thoughts were formed again. They held each other in the strengthening light and whispered words of love and future plans. And it was homecoming.

'Can we have a baby?' Markie whispered yearningly.

Daniel swallowed tightly, aching at the thought. Markie, with his child. 'I'd like that.'

Her face glowed. 'Oh, Daniel, so would I!'

'We'll have to decide where to live,' he told her.

'Here.'

His expression was wary. 'I don't want you to feel as if you're coming to my home. I want it to be *ours*, Markie.'

She smiled at him with such love that he caught his breath. 'I thought we'd settled that.'

'Are you sure?'

'I'm sure. This is where I found love. This is where I belong.'

'We'll build on an office where you can write,' he promised. 'And we'll soundproof it so that the music doesn't bother——'

'No soundproofing, Daniel.' She smiled, and it held peace and happiness and love. 'Like you, I've waited too long for the music.'

EPILOGUE

HE FOUND her sleeping in a meadow of wild flowers—golden pea and violets and wild hyacinth tumbling together in a riot of colour. He thought of it now as *her* meadow, land that belonged to her as surely as his heart did, for she was a part of it all. She belonged to both places, and both to her, for she was soft and somehow strong, like the wild flowers that returned each year, stronger, deeper, purer.

Silently he stretched out on the ground beside her and took her in his arms. Sunlight graced her skin and shimmered in her hair as she slept against him. Even in sleep, he thought with a wonder that never dimmed, she seemed so vibrant. Like the flowers, she was colour and light and all of life to him.

He watched lovingly as a playful breeze tugged a strand of dark hair across her forehead, a single shadow marking her creamy skin. With the touch of a lover and all the longing of the very first time, he brought his lips to her temple. He might as well have danced in flames. . . Through all their months together, the emotion had not muted. Smiling contentedly, Daniel studied his wild flower.

She was even more beautiful now than she had been that day two years ago when he had first found her in the meadow. The strength of their love, the ineffable rightness of belonging had chased the shadows away. She was happy, open, peaceful. She had given all of herself, and, in doing so, taken all of him. Whatever winds might buffet them now stood no chance against the enduring roots that held her to him. And the days were calm. . .

He was different too, he knew. The sanctuary that had eluded him in his earlier days had been found in what they had created together. Like Markie, he was happy, open, peaceful. He had given all of himself, and, in doing so, taken all of her. Whatever demons had driven him in the past were quietly laid to rest with the touch of her hand, the sound of her voice. And the demons had gone. . .

Tightening his arms, he drew her closer, conscious always of the soft swell of her body where their child grew. Soon their son or daughter would be born. Soon there would be three instead of two. Soon their love would produce another life, another piece of belonging.

His wild flower had taken root. . .in love.

**THIS JULY, HARLEQUIN OFFERS YOU
THE PERFECT SUMMER READ!**

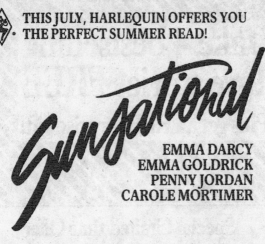

EMMA DARCY
EMMA GOLDRICK
PENNY JORDAN
CAROLE MORTIMER

**From top authors of Harlequin Presents comes
HARLEQUIN SUNSATIONAL, a four-stories-in-one
book with 768 pages of romantic reading.**

Written by such prolific Harlequin authors as Emma Darcy,
Emma Goldrick, Penny Jordan and Carole Mortimer,
HARLEQUIN SUNSATIONAL is the perfect summer
companion to take along to the beach, cottage, on your
dream destination or just for reading at home in the warm
sunshine!

Don't miss this unique reading opportunity.

Available wherever Harlequin books are sold.

Take 4 bestselling love stories FREE

Plus get a FREE surprise gift!

Back by Popular Demand

Janet Dailey
Americana

A romantic tour of America through fifty favorite Harlequin Presents® novels, each set in a different state researched by Janet and her husband, Bill. A journey of a lifetime in one cherished collection.

In June, don't miss the sultry states featured in:

Title # 9 - FLORIDA
   Southern Nights
   #10 - GEORGIA
   Night of the Cotillion

Available wherever Harlequin books are sold.